D0961000

Murder Is for Keeps

ALSO BY ELIZABETH J. DUNCAN

PENNY BRANNIGAN MYSTERY SERIES

Murder on the Hour
Slated for Death
Never Laugh as a Hearse Goes By
A Small Hill to Die On
A Killer's Christmas in Wales
A Brush with Death
The Cold Light of Mourning

SHAKESPEARE IN THE CATSKILLS

Ill Met by Murder
Untimely Death

Murder Is for Keeps

A PENNY BRANNIGAN MYSTERY

Elizabeth J. Duncan

Minotaur Books

A Thomas Dunne Book

New York

This is a work of fiction. All of the characters, organizations, and events portrayed in this novel are either products of the author's imagination or are used fictitiously.

A THOMAS DUNNE BOOK FOR MINOTAUR BOOKS.
An imprint of St. Martin's Press.

www.thomasdunnebooks.com
www.minotaurbooks.com

Library of Congress Cataloging-in-Publication Data

Names: Duncan, Elizabeth J., author.
Title: Murder is for keeps : a Penny Brannigan mystery /
    Elizabeth J. Duncan.
Description: First edition. | New York : Minotaur Books, 2017. |
    Series: A Penny Brannigan mystery ; 8
Identifiers: LCCN 2016048994| ISBN 9781250101471 (hardcover) |
    ISBN 9781250101488 (e-book)
Subjects: LCSH: Brannigan, Penny (Fictitious character)—Fiction. |
    Women private investigators—Fiction. | City and town life—
    Wales—Fiction. | Murder—Investigation—Fiction. | BISAC:
    FICTION / Mystery & Detective / Women Sleuths. | GSAFD:
    Mystery fiction.
Classification: LCC PR9199.4.D863 M865 2017 | DDC 813/.6—dc23
LC record available at https://lccn.loc.gov/2016048994

Our books may be purchased in bulk for promotional, educational, or business use. Please contact your local bookseller or the Macmillan Corporate and Premium Sales Department at 1-800-221-7945, extension 5442, or by e-mail at MacmillanSpecialMarkets@macmillan.com.

First Edition: April 2017

10 9 8 7 6 5 4 3 2 1

For Luci Zahray, the Poison Lady

Acknowledgements

$\mathcal{G}$wrych Castle is a real place. And just as it captured the imagination of the main character in this book, it captured mine. It's a heartbreaking ruin of magnificent proportions located in Abergele, North Wales, and although I may have taken a few liberties with its layout, it is essentially as described here.

Thank you to Dr. Mark Baker, chairman, Gwrych Castle Preservation Trust, for his help with this book, including a guided tour of what remains of the estate. I am in awe of the hardworking volunteers who are restoring what is salvageable, and was delighted to be given the opportunity to donate a Mme. Caroline Testout rose to the reconstruction of the formal garden.

Thank you, also, to the staff at the Llandudno branch of

the Conwy public library system for their assistance with research.

I am grateful to Luci Zahray, a Texas pharmacist who is also a renowned expert on poisons, for her expertise.

And while I strive for accuracy, any errors are mine.

Thank you to my agent, Dominick Abel, editor Melanie Fried, friends Hannah Dennison and Sheila Fletcher for suggested improvements, and my proofreaders, Sylvia and Peter Jones.

I treasure the time spent in North Wales with my son, Lucas Walker, and I'm so glad we were able to explore this stunning property together.

Murder Is for Keeps

One

The slender, fit woman with the red hair picked her way along the rough path, placing her feet carefully to avoid falling. The pathway, with occasional small rocks jutting through the hard-packed, dark soil, was much easier to negotiate now than it had been just a few weeks earlier. Then, it had been choked with weeds and enclosed on both sides by prickly branches and great masses of thorny brambles that had scratched and clawed at her legs.

Burdened with painting supplies in both hands, she was unable to extend her arms for balance so she took her time on the gentle downward slope. At the bottom of the narrow path, she set off on a wider, smoother pathway that led past the main building of Gwrych Castle, an immense late-Georgian castellated mansion. Or what was left of it. Now, it was an abandoned, ruined shell of its former Gothic self, shrouded in decades of neglect but yet somehow maintaining the silent, faded dignity of its long-ago grandeur.

A pointed stone arch draped in ivy, set into an exterior wall that heralded the approach to the castle's main building, beckoned her forward. When she reached it, the woman set down her easel and painting case and pulled a water bottle out of her backpack. It was cooler here in the shade, and she took a long drink as she admired the framed view through the arch. This was as close as she could get to what had been the magnificent manor house of the Bamford-Hesketh family for just three generations, ending with the death of the builder's granddaughter, Winifred, Countess of Dundonald, in 1924. The property then passed out of the family, but was bought by her widower a few years later and then sold in 1946.

The structure was surrounded by tall, strong fencing, clearly marked with red and black DANGER signs. Through the ornate but lifeless cast-iron window frames, the stained glass they once held smashed long ago, she could just make out bits of faded, peeling plaster, and she mourned the loss of what would once have been magnificent, formal rooms. Even from this distance, she could almost smell the damp and decay.

Penny Brannigan had spent the earlier part of the afternoon sketching one of the castle's eighteen towers and now, with the front of the castle bathed in a burst of mid-afternoon sunlight throwing it into stark relief against the heavy shadows of the trees behind it, she made her way down to the main terrace level.

The terrace, with a sweeping, buttressed wall overlooking the parkland below, stretched for two thousand feet along the front of the spread-out conglomerate of buildings that made up the complicated castle site. The wall, like the tops of the towers and many of the buildings, featured a crenellated pattern along the top—notches or indentations that provided a distinctive medieval castle look. She passed a massive cast-iron window frame, all that remained of the conservatory, leaning against a tower and paused to peer over the wall. Below her, the team of workers who had volunteered to clear away decades of weeds and wild overgrowth, some of them still wearing fluorescent lime-green, high-visibility vests, were locking up their tools in a large, dark green metal shipping container.

One of them looked up and upon seeing her, waved.

She raised her hand and waved back. In his early thirties, Mark Baker was an architectural historian and author with a growing reputation and was the driving force behind the restoration work of the castle gardens and the least damaged of the buildings. She'd met him a couple of months ago at an art exhibit opening and was impressed by his dedication and determination. When he'd mentioned an upcoming fund-raising auction, she'd offered to donate a couple of watercolours of the castle, an offer that had been enthusiastically accepted.

The tools and high-viz vests safely stowed until next time, the volunteers changed out of their muddy work boots and Wellies, got in their cars and headed down the rough drive that led to the castle's main gates and lodge, with the busy North Wales Expressway and town of Abergele beyond. Penny turned away from the balustrade and walked on a little farther until she reached her destination, a square, three-storey building called the Melon House, which stood at the western end of the castle.

Named in the 1840s by the Victorian gardeners who grew exotic fruits like melons, grapes, and pineapples within its walls, the Melon House, like the rest of the castle, showed the effects of long-term neglect. Its roof had collapsed, the door was long gone, and the building stood empty, just stone walls and a rough stone floor. Nearby, the dying ashes of a bonfire in which workers had been burning brush continued to smolder.

Penny set up her easel and stool slightly to one side of the building and began to sketch, capturing the simplicity of the building's square symmetry in broad, confident strokes. Half an hour later, satisfied with her work, she tucked the sketch in her carrying case, folded her stool and easel, stood up, and stretched. She shook each leg in turn to work out the stiffness and gathered up her artist's supplies. Although several hours of daylight remained, now that the last of the volunteers had left, she realized she should, too.

The peaceful quiet of a summer's afternoon, broken only by birdsong, had fallen over the estate as she walked to the balustrade to drink in one last time the stunning views of Liverpool Bay and beyond and away to the sparkling waters of the Irish Sea.

She lowered her eyes to the unpaved roadway below her. One vehicle remained. A black pickup truck. She looked to her right, and then turning slowly, surveyed the entire breadth of the castle towers and bastions that ran along the hillside. She saw no movement, no distinctive flash of a fluorescent vest. She saw no one.

She returned to the Melon House and walked round to the back, examining the woodland area of old yew, laurel, and pine trees, but again, saw no one. With a growing sense of unease she returned to the front of the house and once more contemplated the truck. It was unlikely that a volunteer could have fallen or become injured because everyone worked in teams; no one was permitted to work alone. The truck could belong to someone not associated with the work going on here, but because several structures were unsafe, areas were closed off with high metal fencing, stark black-and-white NO ENTRY signs were posted everywhere, and the public wasn't allowed in except on special Open Days or as part of small, accompanied tour groups. She was allowed in to sketch only with Mark's permission and had remained behind today with his approval after the others had left. Of course, vandals and trespassers ignored the signs and entered the grounds all the time, and as the afternoon was drawing to a close, that was another reason for her to leave.

She pulled a pair of small binoculars out of her canvas bag and scanned the grounds one last time, looking for someone who had perhaps stayed behind to finish a task. Except for the extensive canopy of tree branches swaying gently in the July breeze, nothing stirred, until a rusty red blur emerged from the dense woodland behind the castle. It moved with a swift, agile gait, carrying its bushy white-tipped tail horizontal to the ground, as it headed in the direction of the stable yard. A fox, she thought with delight. She hadn't thought of including a fox in her painting, but now that she'd seen one, she would. Deciding there was nothing she could do about the owner of the truck and that it was time to call it a day, she tucked the binoculars back in the bag, gathered up her art supplies, and prepared to set off on the walk to the castle gates to wait for her ride home.

And then, she impulsively decided to see if she could catch a closer glimpse of the fox, so she headed in the other direction, back toward the main building and veered round behind the massive structure into the stable yard. Once a busy part of the operational heart of the estate, the stable yard, or stable court as it was sometimes called, included several connected buildings constructed from the same limestone as the castle. The stables themselves were now open to the elements; the entrances to other buildings, including what had been the blacksmith's workshop and the coach house, were boarded up. Opposite the stables, a small building featured three arched ground-level openings, like half barrels, about shoulder-height. These would once have had metal grilles on the front, and were the original kennels. A perfect place for a fox to hide, or even set up a den, Penny thought. She set her art supplies on the cobblestones, and holding onto the arch at the top of a kennel for support, lowered her head and peered in. It was empty, except for a pile of dead leaves banked against the rough stone wall. She moved on to the next kennel, the middle one.

Something glinted a short distance from the entrance. She leaned over for a closer look. The daylight reached only a little way into the kennel and in the dimness she could just make out the silver stripes on a high-visibility vest. She pulled her mobile phone out of her jacket pocket and crouched into the kennel, covering her mouth against the damp, fetid smell of rotting leaves, aiming the beam of her phone toward the vest. The light was just strong enough to reveal the vest was fastened round a dark shape that looked like a navy blue fleece. She got down on her hands and knees and swept the space with the light from her phone, releasing a frightened gasp when it revealed a head of short brown curls belonging to a figure lying on its side with its back to her. She shook the shoulders gently and said, "Hey! What are you doing in here? Are you all right?" The body of a man rolled slowly onto its back, its open eyes gazing unseeingly at the curved stone roof of the structure.

She crawled backward out of the kennel, sat down heavily on the cobblestones, dialed the police, and waited.

After what seemed an eternity, the distant rise and fall of sirens announced the approach of the North Wales police.

Two

Penny raced round to the front of the castle buildings and hung over the balustrade, waving wildly in the direction of the police vehicle with its blue-and-yellow fluorescent markings as it made its way up the drive. She stayed where she was until recently promoted Det. Inspector Bethan Morgan appeared, accompanied by a uniformed constable.

"Penny," said Bethan, holding out her hand. Penny grasped it with her left hand, pointing in the direction of the stable yard with her right. "Are you all right?" Bethan asked. "It's a terrible shock finding something like that. But I've notified him and he's on his way and he'll be here in a few minutes to take you home."

The "he" Bethan referred to was recently retired Det. Chief Inspector Gareth Davies, who had dropped Penny off at the main gate of Gwrych Castle a couple of hours ago. They'd agreed he would collect her when she was ready to go home, and although he'd offered to pick her up at the volunteer staging area beside the dark green shipping container, she'd insisted she wanted the fifteen-minute walk to the main gate, saying the exercise would do her good. He had suggested a stop at a friendly pub on the drive home to Llanelen and she'd been looking forward to that.

"We can take your statement later, Penny," Bethan said. "But put me in the picture, if you don't mind. Just tell me briefly how you came to find the body." As Penny finished explaining how she'd tried to follow the fox and ended up at the kennels, a tall, fit man in his late fifties entered the stable yard. Gareth Davies put a reassuring arm around Penny's shoulders.

"And there he was," Penny concluded.

"All right?" he asked her. She nodded.

Bethan, as the chief investigating officer, seemed about to say something to him, then caught herself as if she thought better of it. Gareth glanced at the mouth of the kennel, and then turned away. He raised an eyebrow at Bethan and when she nodded, indicating they had her permission to leave, Gareth picked up Penny's art supplies and the two set off.

As they approached his car, Gareth glanced at the black pickup truck that had been parked a little farther down the road, facing the castle gates. He unlocked the passenger door of his vehicle for Penny, and when she was seated, told her he'd be right back.

He headed toward the truck and without touching it, walked slowly round it, peering in each window.

He then turned his gaze up to the sweep of the castle buildings and finally returned to his own car.

"I expect you've been here before," Penny said as he got in.

"Oh, yes, many times," he said as he started the car. "I was brought here in the 1960s when I was a boy. It wasn't in such a ruinous state, of course. In fact, it had been turned into one of Wales's top tourist attractions, although there was something sad and undignified about that—like making a beautiful animal do something unnatural in a garish costume. Bears riding bicycles. Elephants giving rides to tourists. That sort of thing. A miniature train gave kiddy rides, there was a chamber of horrors and even jousting tournaments. The sorts of activities that passed as a great day out for the family, back in the day. And what had once been the library was converted into a sleazy nightclub at some point. And visitors were allowed to wander all over the house. One room, I remember, had a clockwork canary in a little cage. You put a sixpence in the slot and the canary would sing. Can't remember who owned the property at the time, but it passed out of family ownership just after the war, I believe. Such a shame it was allowed to fall into this terrible state of disrepair."

"That's what everybody says when you mention Gwrych Castle. 'What a shame.' Heartbreaking, really. Especially when you compare it to other properties of the same age that have been beautifully and lovingly maintained."

She turned round in her seat to look back at the castle as they drove off. "It's a very romantic style," said Penny, resuming a forward-facing position. "In older photographs you can see how lovely it was. And I really like the way it's laid out in a linear style, not square. The way it's set into the hillside and just goes on and on, a chain of towers, walls, and buildings."

"Of course, it's not really a castle," said Gareth. "At least not in that medieval meaning of a fortified residence for a king. It's one of those magnificent country houses built by very wealthy people."

"Do you know much about its history?"

"A little. I have a personal connection to it."

"Oh, right. I suppose as a police officer you were called out here many times. Vandals and trespassers and so on."

"Well, yes, there is that. But my real connection to the property is family. My grandmother came here when she was fifteen to work as a seamstress. She hemmed the sheets, embroidered the monograms on the linen, made quilts, and mended the family's clothes."

He broke off speaking as he downshifted for a turn and checked for oncoming traffic.

"You can imagine how important this estate once was to the local economy, both while it was being built and afterward, in the running of it. It was like a self-sustaining town. There was even a brewery."

"Did your grandmother tell you much about what life was like here? It must have been wonderfully grand in its heyday."

"She probably tried to talk to me about it, but I'm afraid I wasn't really interested. Boys don't care about that sort of thing, do they? Of course, now that I'd really like to hear about it, she's gone." He glanced at his companion. "What would you like to do now? Do you still want to stop in at the pub, or would you rather just go home?"

"I think I'd just like to go home."

"Right. I'm sorry your painting excursion ended so unpleasantly."

"Me, too. I was enjoying it. I do so many landscapes; the castle's buildings and walls make a nice change. I like the challenge of getting the perspective right."

Half an hour later they pulled up in front of Penny's cottage on the edge of Llanelen, a picturesque market town in North Wales. Gareth carried in her painting supplies, set them down in the entranceway, and held out his arms.

"It's a real shock, finding a body like that," he said over the top of her head, and then released her. "Can I get you a brandy?"

She shook her head. "No, just a cup of tea."

"You sit down, get comfortable, and I'll make it."

She led the way into the sitting room and sat on the sofa while Gareth continued on into the kitchen and rattled about with the tea things. He returned a few minutes later and set the tray on the low table in front of the sofa, poured a cup and handed it to her.

She accepted it with a smile. "I guess when you spend a long time in the police service you learn how to make a decent cup of tea."

He returned her smile. "I guess you do."

"I thought I picked up something with Bethan today outside the kennel. It was almost as if she wanted to ask you to have a look at the body."

Gareth took a sip of tea and helped himself to a biscuit.

"I almost found myself offering to have a look," he said.

"I certainly wanted to. Had to remind myself that it's not my case, she's in charge and I'm retired. Although I have to admit, I would have liked to see it."

"Still, I suppose if she needs your help she can ask for it," Penny said.

Gareth raised a hand in a small gesture that might have been dismissive, or might have been merely agreement.

"She can ask, and if she gets stuck, I'm sure she will. She's ambitious and she'll do what it takes to get the right result. She won't let any false pride about asking me or anyone else for help get in the way. She'll just want to come out of this looking good."

Penny nibbled at a biscuit. "It's always intrigued me. The castle. You drive along the A55 and see it set up there in its woodland. How I wish I could have seen it back in the day, before all the neglect. Places like that—and there are far too many of them—have a certain melancholic beauty." She sighed. "When I'm there, I can picture what it must have been like when it was thriving. People bustling about their work, maybe a groom and a pretty dairy maid passing in the stable yard, hoping to catch a few minutes together at the end of the day." She laughed. "I know. I'm such a romantic but you must admit the place itself is romantic."

"Oh, it is," Gareth agreed.

"And the expanse of it. The way the buildings spread out, on and on, nestled into the hillside, set so high up." She held up two hands in front of her, together, then moved her arms apart in a sweeping gesture. "It's hard to describe. My paintings will never do it justice. It's got something that's impossible to capture. The play of light on all that greenery and the complexity of the ruined buildings. . . .

"And I so admire what all the volunteers are doing. They're working so hard to clear away all the undergrowth and replant the gardens and the work they've done is impressive." She shook her head. "But I don't think the buildings will ever be restored. I know from the renovation we did on the Spa how quickly everything adds up and our building is just a tiny fraction of that one."

A couple of years ago Penny and her friend and business partner, Victoria Hopkirk, renovated a rundown stone building by the river and converted it into a stylish, contemporary space that maintained the building's character and charm. The Llanelen Spa had turned out to be a successful business of which both women were justifiably proud.

"No, I think what Gwrych Castle once was, is lost forever. Oh, there's been talk over the years of turning it into a grand hotel or an opera house or a conference centre. But it would just be the most awful money pit, and besides, is another conference centre or wedding venue needed around here?"

"You're right about that," said Gareth as he gathered up the tea things. "Should we be thinking about dinner? Are you getting hungry?"

"A little, maybe. But I certainly don't feel like cooking and I don't feel like going out."

"We'll order in then and I'll pick it up."

Gareth carried the tea tray through to the kitchen. He returned to find Penny stretched out on the sofa, so he lowered himself into an adjacent wing chair, and sat facing her.

"If you feel like talking about it," he said, swinging one leg over the other and settling back, "you'll find me a good listener."

"Talk about what?" she said with her eyes closed.

"Finding the body."

"What would you like to know?"

"Everything."

Three

So you didn't hear or see anything that made you suspicious?" Gareth asked when Penny had finished describing the events of the afternoon. "Nothing that you now, with hindsight, question or wonder about?"

Penny smiled as she answered with a simple no, then added, "It's not your case but part of you wishes it was. Am I right in thinking that?"

It was Gareth's turn to smile. "I'm an old dog on a long road." He rubbed his chin. "Well, I don't suppose there's much more to be done until they find out who the victim is and how he died, so we might as well think about dinner."

"Good idea."

"You know, Penny," Gareth said as he stood up, "it's a bit troubling to me that you don't seem at all upset by what happened this afternoon. Of course, a discovery like that affects people differently. Some people who find a dead body are very shaken by it and the horror of it stays with them for years. Or the rest of their lives, even. But you don't seem very bothered right now, so you should be prepared that you may have a delayed reaction."

"I didn't actually see too much. It was quite dark in there and although I touched the body, well, shook it, I didn't feel close to it. I didn't see any blood or gore, or anything like that, so as these things go, I suppose it wasn't too bad, really."

"Yes, I suppose that could account for it. But it may come back to haunt you later, or you might find yourself having flashbacks, and if you do, let me know and we'll arrange some help for you."

"You do know that you still sound exactly like a policeman, don't you?" said Penny as she swung her legs over the side of the sofa and sat up. "I think you're going to find retirement a little more challenging than you thought."

"Oh, I don't know," said Gareth. "There's always gardening. And you, of course. I'm hoping you'll find lots of things for me to do. I thought I'd make a start by having a look at that awful squeak in the gate at the Spa."

Penny laughed. "Oh, would you? We've been waiting ages for a handy fellow like you to come along and sort it out."

"Right, well, tell me what you fancy for dinner and I'll order and pick it up," Gareth said.

"How do you feel about Thai?"

But their dinner thoughts were interrupted by the sound of tires crunching to a stop on the gravel outside the window. Det. Inspector Bethan Morgan got out of the driver's side of a marked police vehicle accompanied by her uniformed constable.

Gareth raised a questioning eyebrow and on Penny's nod, he opened the door.

"Bethan," he said. "And PC Chris Jones. Come in."

They entered the sitting room and Penny indicated a pair of comfortable chairs. "Can I offer you anything?" she asked.

"Just some water, thanks. It's been a hot afternoon."

Gareth fetched them each a glass and Bethan took a grateful sip.

"Well, this is a little different," she said with a smile, looking from one to the other. "In the old days it would have been the DCI and me on the same team asking the questions." She set her glass of water down and nodded at the constable, who opened his notebook. "Right. Well, just to give you a quick update and then I'd like to take Penny's statement. It may be that she now remembers a bit more than what she was able to tell us earlier."

"I'll do my best," said Penny.

"So we've made a little progress," said Bethan. "Our deceased gentleman is called John Hardwick. He's a fifty-five-year-old landscape architect who lives just outside Llanelen. We're on our way to speak to his wife. She hasn't identified him formally, but from the identification he had on him, we're pretty sure that's who he is."

"So if he's a landscape architect, was he working on the Gwrych garden project?" asked Penny.

"His wife may be able to tell us that."

"How did he die?" Gareth asked.

"That's an important detail we don't know yet. There were no obvious signs of trauma to the body. And nothing

19

to indicate suicide. The pathologist isn't sure yet exactly what happened, but we should know more after the post-mortem. So in the meantime, we're treating his death as unexplained. It's early days, as you know."

Gareth nodded. "Of course. But where the body was found will have made it difficult to get much information in situ. I wonder if he died there, or if the body was moved."

"That's what I'm thinking. We didn't find any marks that would indicate the body was dragged, but it's hard to tell on cobblestones." She checked her watch and looked hopefully at Penny.

"We were just about to get some Thai food if you'd like to stay and join us for dinner," said Penny, taking the hint. "Gareth was going to pick it up."

"I was," he agreed. "I could do that and you could perhaps take Penny's statement while I'm gone and get that out of the way."

"Sounds good to me," said Bethan, as Gareth prepared to leave. "You can tell me what happened, Penny, and I'll get it typed up and you can drop by the station tomorrow and sign it. Start with the time and what you were doing up there at the castle and include everything you did and saw."

Penny sighed, and told her story one more time.

"And how many times have you been painting at the castle, Penny?" Bethan asked when she was finished.

"Four or five. I'm still working on the sketches."

"And did you ever see or talk to Mr. Hardwick when you were up there?"

"No. But I'd have no reason to. They were working on the garden or whatever and I'm not part of that."

Four

Penny enjoyed walking to work, especially in summer. As she walked along the river the next morning, watching it splash and dance in the sunshine, the events of yesterday seemed distant and almost as if they'd happened to someone else. Or as if she'd been a dispassionate observer, silent and unseen, watching the discovery of the body unfold. She'd thought about what Gareth had said about her having so little reaction to it afterward, but then he hadn't been there at the awful moment when she discovered the body. The pounding heart, surging adrenaline, dry mouth, she'd experienced it all. The fear, both of the body and that the killer, if there was one, might still be nearby. And thinking about it now, she started to feel some of the same heightened emotion and found her legs weren't working quite as well as they had been a minute earlier.

Muttering, "Pull yourself together," she strode on until she arrived at the graceful three-arched bridge that symbolized the town, crossed the street and swung open the black wrought-iron gate that separated the pavement from the little path that led to the Spa's entrance. As the gate squeaked open, she smiled to herself. Gareth was right. That gate needed attention.

She opened the door to the Spa, greeted Rhian Phillips, the receptionist, and walked to her office, popping her head into her partner's office as she passed. Victoria Hopkirk, who lived in the apartment on the top floor of the Spa, was almost always at her desk when Penny arrived, but this morning, she wasn't.

Penny continued on to her own office, checked her e-mail, and then walked to the manicure salon at the end of the hallway where her assistant, Eirlys, was setting up for the first appointment of the day. Penny checked the client list.

"It looks as if we'll be busy," she said to Eirlys. "Mrs. Lloyd'll be here in a few minutes."

As she finished speaking a woman in her sixties with tightly permed grey hair entered.

"Morning, Penny. Eirlys," she said, nodding at each. "Not late am I?"

"No," said Eirlys. "Right on time as usual."

"Well, that's good, then," said Mrs. Lloyd, easing herself into the client's chair. While Eirlys filled the soaking basin with warm, lavender-scented water, Mrs. Lloyd gave Penny a sly smile.

"I guess you heard all about that unfortunate business up at Gwrych Castle yesterday," she said.

"You mean the body that was discovered? Yes, I more than heard about it," said Penny. "I was there."

"Never!" said Mrs. Lloyd, dipping her fingers in the basin and nodding at Eirlys to indicate the water temperature was just the way she liked it. "Whatever happened? Tell me all about it."

Penny kept the answer simple. "I was up there sketching and came upon a body in a little space that might once have been a dog kennel." Eirlys's eyebrows shot up and Mrs. Lloyd leaned forward in her chair.

"Put like that, it does sound strange, I agree," said Penny. "But that's what happened."

"Why is it always you who gets involved in the murders, Penny?" asked Eirlys.

"Yes, I've often wondered that myself," said Mrs. Lloyd. "You do have a certain knack for finding bodies and getting caught up in the investigation. Although I suppose that's not going to happen anymore, now that your police inspector gentleman friend has retired. At least not to the same extent."

"I expect not," said Penny, "although to be fair, Eirlys, we don't know for sure that there was a murder. Apparently the police found no signs of foul play. Or that he committed suicide, so they're classifying it as unexplained."

Eirlys began shaping the fingernails on Mrs. Lloyd's right hand and the two of them looked expectantly at Penny.

"There is one thing, Mrs. Lloyd," Penny said. "The deceased man. John Hardwick. I wondered if you know anything about him?"

Mrs. Lloyd looked at her in surprise. "Did you say John Hardwick? Good heavens!"

"Well, yes, didn't you know that's who it was? I thought the name would have been on the news by now. I know the police planned to speak to the family last night, so there doesn't seem to be any reason for the name to be withheld."

"Oh, my goodness!" said Mrs. Lloyd again. "He lives just outside town. Lived, I guess I should say. Moved here, oh, must be fifteen years ago. I was still working at the post office, at any rate. There was some talk at the time about why he'd left his job." She shrugged. "Well, there's always that kind of talk, isn't there, when someone leaves a really good job to come here and do what?"

"What kind of job did he have that was so wonderful?" Eirlys asked.

"Oh, he was something or other in the Royal Parks service. Practically worked for the Queen. It was his job to cut down trees at Windsor Castle or some such thing."

"The Queen herself," breathed Eirlys.

"Well, it's not as if Her Majesty personally stood there in her Wellies overseeing his work, you understand, Eirlys dear," said Mrs. Lloyd. "But I heard he was high up and every now and then an envelope would arrive for him with royal franking on it. You don't see that every day, so that's why I remembered him."

"Did you know him at all?" asked Penny, reaching into a wicker basket and pulling out a pile of white towels that needed folding.

"Well, I knew him when he came into the post office. A little on the condescending side, you might say. Expected everybody else in the queue to give way for him because he was so much busier and his time so much more precious than theirs."

"And did they?" asked Eirlys.

"Did they like as heck!" She paused for a moment, as if recollecting John Hardwick in the queue in her post office.

"There was something pushy about him. He seemed to want a lot of attention." She turned to Eirlys and said something in Welsh that Penny didn't understand. Eirlys replied a moment later. "That's it," said Mrs. Lloyd. "We have an expression in Welsh for it and I was just asking Eirlys if she could think of it."

"*Ceffyl blaen,*" said Eirlys. "It translates something like 'the horse in front.'" She looked to Mrs. Lloyd for support. "I'm not sure I can explain it properly."

"It means the showiest horse, the one with the fanciest bridle, maybe the one with plumage on top of his head, the one seeking all the attention," said Mrs. Lloyd. "The one who prances along out front demanding that all eyes be on him. The one who really enjoys being in the spotlight."

"Oh, I see," said Penny. "At least, I think I do. Interesting expression. I'm not sure we have anything quite like it in English."

"We have lots of expressions in Welsh that you don't have in English," said Mrs. Lloyd. "But never mind that now. Very full of himself, John Hardwick was. He and his wife came out once or twice to join us at the bridge games, but fortunately that didn't last long. She was all right, I suppose, but no one wanted to play with him. Always criticizing his partner and opponents and pulling a card out of his hand and tapping it on the table before it was his turn to play. Odious man! We were glad to see the back of him."

"How long ago was this, Mrs. Lloyd?" asked Penny.

"Oh, a good few years ago now."

"Where did they live before they moved here, do you know? Windsor, did you say?"

"Well, I'm not sure, but probably on some royal estate where they have a lot of trees."

Penny laughed. "I think that would include all of them."

Mrs. Lloyd joined in good-naturedly. "Yes, I guess so." As the laughter faded, she commented, "But still, just because nobody particularly liked him isn't reason enough for him to get killed. If he was killed, of course. You say that we don't know that for sure. But it all seems very peculiar to me."

Penny folded and smoothed the last hand towel, handed it to Eirlys, and set the rest to one side. After touching Mrs. Lloyd lightly on the shoulder, Penny said, "Well, I'll leave you to it."

She walked down the hall and seeing that Victoria had arrived, popped into her office. Victoria looked up from her computer and smiled.

"Morning, Penny. I hear you've got yourself involved in another crime. How does it happen, I ask myself, that you always seem to be on the scene when these things occur? Someone more suspicious than I am might wonder why that is."

Penny laughed. "Oh, not you, too. I just heard practically the same thing from Mrs. Lloyd. But it was nothing to do with me, I can assure you. I didn't even know the man. And anyway, the police aren't even sure yet there was a crime."

"What are you going to do now? Not rushing off to investigate, I hope."

"That's why I popped in to see you. I have to go to the

police station this morning and sign the statement that Bethan took last night. Eirlys is taking care of Mrs. Lloyd, so I thought now might be a good time. Just wanted to let you know I'll be out for a bit."

"Right. See you when you get back."

"It all seems very peculiar." Penny reflected on Mrs. Lloyd's words as she walked up Station Road. She passed the public library and entered the small police station where Bethan had said she'd be working today. Penny was shown into an interview room, bare except for a table and chair bolted to the floor and audio recording equipment on the table beside the wall. Bethan followed her in and when they were seated, opened a legal-size manila folder and slid a typed form across the table.

"I typed up your statement based on the notes I took at the castle and at your residence last evening, Penny," she said. "If you agree with it, sign it. If you want to add or delete anything, we can do that." Penny read over the statement and then held out her hand for a pen. When she had signed, she closed the folder and slid it back across the desk to Bethan, saying, "Mrs. Lloyd says she knew the victim and he wasn't very popular."

"No, it seems he wasn't very well liked. We've just started looking into his past but so far, besides his wife, no one seems very sorry he's dead. It does seem he rubbed a lot of people round here the wrong way."

"Yes, but rubbing people the wrong way doesn't usually get you killed," said Penny. "If he was killed, of course. There has to be more to it."

"Oh, definitely. And finding out what more there is to

it is exactly what we intend to do." Was there the slightest emphasis on the word "we," Penny wondered.

Bethan stood up and held out her hand. "Well, mustn't keep you. Thanks for coming in. I'll walk you out."

"If I think of anything else, I'll let you know."

"Yes, you do that. You've got my number."

Penny found herself outside the station almost before she knew what was happening. She stood on the pavement, looking at the modern, charmless, brown brick structure and thought that Bethan had been unusually fast and formal. Her use of that police jargon phrase "at your residence last evening." She shrugged it off, thinking Bethan was probably just in the midst of a wildly busy day. She glanced at the adjacent library, hesitated for a moment, and then went in.

Librarian Jean Bryson stood behind the desk engaged in an animated conversation with Florence Semble. Florence had started out as Mrs. Lloyd's boarder, and then become what Mrs. Lloyd liked to think of as her companion.

"Oh, I didn't see it that way at all," Jean was saying. "I think we were meant to think that, but . . ." She stopped and the women offered Penny warm hellos in the form of broad smiles. "Sorry, Penny, we were just discussing a program on telly last night. The conclusion is tonight and Florence and I disagree on who the killer is."

"It's Mrs. Nixon," said Florence. "There's something shifty about her that I don't like. And her eyes are too close together and a bit on the squinty side." Jean laughed. "No, it's the vicar. It was the hymn choice that gave him away. You'll see!"

"Well, I'm sure one of you is right," Penny said. "Or maybe they were in on it together and you're both right!"

Jean cleared her throat and checked her watch. "Was there something I can help you with, Penny? Florence and I were just about to take our picnic lunches into the church-yard."

"Oh, right," said Penny. "Well, I won't keep you. I just popped in to see if you have any books on Gwrych Castle."

"We do, but the best one is reference only," she said. "We don't have a circulating copy. I'll show you where it is." She led Penny to the local history section, crouched down, and using her index finger as a pointer, worked her way along the call numbers on the spines of the books. She went back and forth between a couple of books and then widened her search to include a few more books in each direction.

"That's funny," she said, straightening up. "It doesn't seem to be here. Nobody else asked for it today, but I'll check to see if it's been left on a table. It's a slim volume with a red cover." She lifted up a couple of opened news-papers and peered under them. When she moved on, Florence picked up the papers, folded them, and stacked them neatly on a corner of the table. "Doesn't seem to be here," said Jean, crossing her arms. "And that's odd because now that I think about it, someone else was in here recently asking for that very book and I know it was reshelved properly because I did it myself. Sometimes readers mean to be help-ful but they put the books back in the wrong place. We really would rather they just leave the books on the tables for us to deal with." She sighed. "I'm sorry, but it doesn't seem to be here. Of course, it could turn up and if it does,

I'll ring you. Otherwise, I could try to order one from another branch for you."

"That's all right," said Penny. "If you tell me the name of the book and the author, I'll buy one."

"Well, it's *The Rise and Fall of Gwrych Castle* by Mark Baker but I don't think you'll be able to buy one. The other person who was in here looking at the book said they'd tried everywhere to find even a used copy for sale, but apparently it's out of print and you can't get one for love nor money."

"Mark! Of course, I should have known he'd have written a book about the castle. He's our local expert on it." She let out a little sigh of frustrated disappointment.

"Oh, damn, I'd love to see it. This other person who was looking at the book," she continued, "could you tell me who he or she was?"

"I'm sorry," said Jean. "I can't. Because it's a reference book and anyone can use the library I had no reason to ask the person's name. And besides," she added with an apologetic shrug, "even if I had checked the book out and could remember the person's name, library confidentiality policy wouldn't let me tell you. Just as I couldn't tell anyone that you were in here today looking for it. I'm sure you understand."

"Of course," said Penny, wondering if the policy would remain in force if the police were asking the question. "Well, in that case, then, perhaps there's another copy available in the library system?"

"There should be several," said Jean. "You could try another branch. Or as I said, I could order one in for you."

"No, that's all right. I don't want to keep you any longer and besides, I may be able to borrow one right from the source. I know Mark and he might be able to lend me a copy. And in the meantime, there's always Google."

"Tell me again how you pronounce the name of that castle place," said Florence, "and how do you spell it?" Penny spelled it out and pronounced it slowly. "GOO–RE–K. A bit like Zurich with a G."

"I thought it was pronounced 'Gritch,' but what do I know?" Florence repeated the name a couple of times following Penny's instructions and seemed pleased with the way it sounded.

"It means hedge, by the way, *gwrych* does. I wonder if that's because the massive stone wall that runs along the castle is almost like a stone hedge," said Penny. "It's even got buttresses holding it up, that's how massive it is. A craftsman's work of art, when you think about it."

"It is, indeed. Well, if there's nothing else, then, Penny, we'd best be off," said Jean. "I only get an hour for lunch and we do want to make the most of this lovely day."

"Yes, we certainly do," agreed Florence. "Are you going to the Spa now, Penny?"

Realizing that Florence was only asking to be polite, and that if she said yes, the three of them would have to walk together in some awkwardness to the town square, and sensing that Jean preferred to be alone with Florence, Penny replied, "No, actually, I thought I'd browse the local history section and see if there's anything else that might have a chapter or two on the castle and then maybe use a computer for a few minutes."

Jean did her best to hide a relieved smile, and she and Florence set off.

Penny signed onto a computer and began to scroll through pages of information on Gwrych Castle. As she did so, she asked herself the question that detectives often ask themselves as they begin to piece together the events that led to murder.

Why here? Why was this person murdered here? If he was murdered, that is, she reminded herself. We don't know that.

Within a few minutes she had disappeared into the vanished world that was Gwrych Castle. Immersed in her reading, she forgot about the time until a small sound behind her caught her attention. She turned to see two boys, one quite a bit older than the other, setting up a game of chess on the table. The older boy rotated the board that the younger boy had set down. "The white square always goes in the lower right corner," he said. When the game was set up, they drew pawns to see who would go first and the game began. Now cognizant of the time, and aware that she'd been away from the Spa longer than she'd intended, Penny gathered up her things and left.

While their work at the Spa kept her and Victoria busy, it also afforded them flexibility in their working lives. Penny enjoyed days off to sketch and ramble, and Victoria, an accomplished harpist, gave occasional afternoon performances at the local nursing home and at genteel tearooms looking to offer a bit more atmosphere. So she can't be too cross with me for being gone a little longer than I meant to, Penny thought as she walked purposefully down Station Road.

Five

"I expect the police will look into the backgrounds of all the volunteers who were working at the castle yester-day," said Penny at dinner that night.

"You can be sure of that," Gareth replied. "It's a good place to begin eliminating people from the inquiry."

"When you say inquiry, do you think he was killed?"

"I don't know. I didn't get to see the body, remember? But until they have some answers, the police will continue to categorize the death as unexplained and keep an open mind about it." He folded his arms on the table and leaned forward. "I must admit it still feels strange saying 'the police' and not 'we.' Just something I'll have to get used to, I guess."

"I wonder why he died there, though. In that place. In that dog kennel."

"Well, he could have died from natural causes. Maybe he had a heart attack. He could have gone in there to look for something and it happened. Heart attacks can happen anytime, anywhere. And don't forget there's also the mis-adventure category. He could have died from an accident. Maybe he misjudged the height of the kennel, banged his head, and that was it. Although, if that happened, you'd expect there to be blood or some kind of wound. Really, speculation doesn't get us anywhere. The best thing to do is wait and see what the postmortem examination reveals. If the results are inconclusive, the police will keep the case open. If it turns out he did die from, say, natural causes, then, well, that's your answer and case closed."

"I hope it does turn out he died from natural causes," said Penny. "It's just that when you find a body like that, you tend to assume the worst, don't you."

"I guess you do."

Penny was silent for a moment. "Still," she said, "I want to learn more about the castle and its history. Mark Baker's written a book about it and I tried to get my hands on a copy at the library today, but it may have gone missing. Someone else was apparently interested in it, too. I've scoured all the online sites that sell used books and Mark's book is out of print and unobtainable but it wouldn't hurt to ask if he's got a spare copy he'd be willing to lend me."

"You're falling under the spell of the place," said Gareth, "and goodness knows, that's easy enough to do and you wouldn't be the first. There's definitely something about it that draws people in."

"One can only imagine how stunning it must have been

when the family lived there. When the gardens were filled with beautiful flowers, the rooms were furnished . . . the stained glass windows . . . the stunning views down to the sea . . . it was loved and cared for . . . how idyllic and romantic it must have all been. . . ."

Gareth and Penny's relationship was not romantic. They'd met several years ago when he was investigating the murder of a posh bride, and over time, had become close. However, at times each had wanted different things from the relationship and they had effectively broken up a few months ago. Now, they were back together in a comfortable, friendly arrangement that seemed to be working well. Penny had made it clear she did not want to marry him and would not consider moving out of her cosy cottage. Neither did she want him to move in with her. She valued her space, her independence, and she needed time alone. She wanted him in her life, but only as a dear friend. And after all, their friendship seemed to be working well, with an occasional show of affection, so why try to make it into something it wasn't?

He, on the other hand, would have loved to marry her, but if friendship was all she could offer, he'd settle for that.

"When I stopped in at the police station to sign the statement I thought Bethan seemed just a little, oh, I don't know, resistant to any help," Penny said. "She just seemed to want me to know that the police would handle everything, thank you very much."

Gareth grinned. "That's just her letting you know that she's in charge. She needs to assert her authority. And there's not that much to handle at this stage. But if and when this turns into a bigger investigation and she runs out of steam, she'll be glad enough of any help we can offer to get her lines of inquiry up and running again. You'll see."

"Does it bother you talking about the police investigation? I hope I'm not making you uncomfortable."

"Well, I'm retired, so it's got nothing to do with me, has it?" he said. "At least that's what I keep telling myself. What's that popular expression? 'Not my circus. Not my monkey.'"

Penny laughed. "Well, speaking of monkey, apparently there are monkey puzzle trees in the Gwrych gardens. What a strange name for a tree. Fun, though."

"Chilean pine is its more proper name."

"How do you know that?"

"I do know a thing or two about British gardens. And I say that in the most humble way. There's so much more I don't know."

After dinner, Penny called Mark who told her he planned to be on site at the castle in the morning, if she wanted to meet him there and pick up a copy of his book. "I wouldn't mind having a closer look at the garden," Gareth said, offering to drive her.

And so the next morning, as the sun lit up the vast greenery that enrobed the castle buildings, Gareth and Penny drove under the arch that marked the main entryway to Gwrych Castle.

A massive pair of round towers, joined by a corbelled overhang that continued the romantic battlemented theme of all the buildings, formed the entrance. Beyond these gates lay a five-hundred-acre park, surrounded by a complete boundary limestone wall, with the main house itself and all the outbuildings at the centre.

Gareth parked beside the green shipping container where the tools were stored. The door to the container was open, revealing a wall lined with racks of every kind of gardening implement.

A tall, slim man, auburn hair cut short on the sides and back with a floppy quiff, approached them from the other side of the container.

Penny introduced Gareth to Mark Baker and the two men shook hands.

"I hear it was you who found the body of John Hardwick," Mark said to Penny. "That must have been traumatic." She nodded. "We haven't been told much about it, but hopefully there'll be more information soon."

"Had he been working up here long?" Gareth asked.

"Only about six weeks or so, I believe."

Gareth turned away and surveyed the broad expanse of cleared land at the base of the wall that ran along the frontage of the castle buildings.

"That's an ambitious undertaking," he remarked.

"It is," agreed Mark. "It's taken our team a couple of years to get this much done. They had to clear thirty or forty years' worth of vigorous overgrowth. We've removed self-seeding trees, winter heliotrope, masses of ivy, brambles, branches, and even deadly nightshade. Literally, tons of it. But we're gradually starting to see the layout of the gardens as they were in the 1920s. There's a watercolour that was painted about that time and we'll be asking a botanist to help us determine what kinds of flowers were planted, so we can re-create it."

"I'm impressed," said Gareth. "The team's doing a great job."

"Yes, they are. But we've still got a long way to go. This is a huge, never-ending job."

"Gareth's grandmother worked here," said Penny.

"Really?" said Mark, his face lighting up. "When? What was her name?"

"Her maiden name was Annie Evans," said Gareth. "She started working here as a seamstress when she was only fifteen. I'm not sure of the exact dates but I think she might have made clothes for the children of the family."

Mark sized Gareth up and frowned. "Not sure she would have sewed for the children as they probably would have been older when your grandmother worked here. But if you give me her dates, we could work it out. A few of the old estate books still exist. I could see if she's in them, if you'd like. The estate managers kept detailed records of the staff and their duties, how long they were here, how much they were paid, and so on."

"Oh, that would be interesting," said Gareth. "She died in 1994 and never really talked much about the time she worked here. I would have liked to hear about it."

"I'd like to look into it. I'm always interested in hearing stories of the people who lived and worked here," said Mark. "By all accounts the countess treated all her staff very well. I've seen a record that indicated the seamstresses were given a special workroom on the first floor, not below stairs, because the light was better and it was thought it would be easier on their eyes."

As he finished speaking, a short, stocky man carrying a mug of tea emerged from a small shed beside the shipping container and Mark introduced him as Ifor Jones, the site manager who was also in charge of volunteers. Jones pulled off a pair of work gloves and then brushed a lock of curly grey hair out of his eyes with a stubby, dirty hand and glanced at Gareth and Penny. Without really acknowledging them, he spoke to Mark Baker in a deep, gravelly voice.

"I'd hoped to get the lads working on clearing the debris out of the stables. Do you know how much longer the police are going to have the area cordoned off?"

"They said it wouldn't be too long," Mark replied, "but I don't know for sure."

"I could ask for you, if you like," offered Gareth. "If this death had happened here a month ago," he gestured toward the buildings above them, "it would have been me looking into it."

"He's just retired from the police," Penny chimed in. "Detective Chief Inspector."

"Oh, right," said Mark, "well, yes, if you could find out, that would be appreciated. We're keen to get on with clearing. We've got what we call an Open Day coming up in early September and we want the place looking as good as possible by then. Along with the auction, it's one of our main fund-raisers."

As Gareth stepped away, holding his phone to his ear, Mark and Ifor exchanged a glance that Penny couldn't quite read, but had seen before when people learned he was a senior police officer. Mark's slight shaking of his head, accompanied by a narrowing of his eyes could have been a, 'be careful what you say' kind of warning. Then again, perhaps it had nothing to do with Gareth.

"The detective inspector who's in charge of the case just happens to be on her way over right now," Gareth said as he rejoined Penny and the two men. "She's asked you both to meet her here." He turned to Penny. "She said there's no need for us to stick around."

"Are we leaving now, then?" asked Penny.

"Yes, I think we'd better be on our way."

"Well, in that case, Mark, I wondered if you were able to find that copy of your book you so kindly . . ."

Mark grimaced. "Oh, I'm so sorry. I didn't make it home last night, so I wasn't able to get it for you. To be honest, it completely slipped my mind. Sorry you've had a wasted journey."

"Oh, no, not at all. Coming here is never wasted."

"I will get that book to you, I promise. In the meantime, I hope you'll be back soon to carry on with the sketching. It's very good of you to do those paintings for us. Just be sure to let me know when you're coming on site."

Gareth extended his hand to Mark. "I'd like to come back another day, too, and have a closer look at the garden work, if that would be all right. This just doesn't seem like the right time. I can see you've both got a lot going on."

"That would be fine," said Mark as he shook the proffered hand, "but only when someone's here. If I'm not here, Ifor will look after you. The steps are worn and can be slippery and there are lots of no-go areas. It's for your protection, and ours. There's the insurance to worry about and you know what the health and safety people are like."

"Indeed I do." Gareth cast a mildly appraising look over Ifor Jones, and then said, "Right, well, I guess we'll be off."

As Gareth and Penny drove down the main drive, a police car entered the gates and proceeded toward them. Both vehicles slowed to pass and Gareth lowered his window, expecting to exchange a few words with his former sergeant. But she did not lower her window and after a brief wave and smile, she resumed speed and drove on.

"Well," said Gareth as he raised the window. "I think she's just sent me the same message she gave you yesterday."

Gareth glanced at the gate towers as they passed under the archway, checked for oncoming traffic, and then pulled onto the main road. "Did you notice Jones was wearing brand-new work gloves? Now, if this had been my case, that fact would interest me. Why new gloves just now? And I wonder if Bethan's had forensics examine that bonfire they had going on the day the body was discovered. It would be very telling to me if they found burned bits of old gloves in it."

"Not being part of this investigation is killing you, isn't it?" said Penny.

Gareth laughed. "It is. I didn't think I'd feel this way. I thought I'd be happy to sit back and let Bethan get on with it, but now I'm not so sure."

"What aren't you sure about?"

"I'm not sure she's—this is hard to say—it's not that I think she isn't up to the job. She is, or I wouldn't have recommended her for promotion. She's a good detective and someday she'll probably be a great one. I'm just not sure that she's ready to take on the responsibility of leading a murder investigation team."

"It may be that she just doesn't have the confidence yet," said Penny. "She learned a lot from you. It might have been

41

better if she'd been able to work a few more cases under your direction."

"I don't know," said Gareth. "I thought she was ready and that's one of the reasons I decided to retire when I did, but maybe you're right and I did leave a case or two too soon."

"Perhaps she was ready, or at least appeared ready, because she was still working with you," said Penny. "But without you, she's a bit unsure of herself. Once she gets her feet under her and gets a good result behind her, and with her confidence up and running, she'll be fine." He glanced at Penny, then returned his eyes to the road ahead.

"Bethan should have a clearer idea what she's dealing with soon. I imagine the postmortem results will be delivered today or tomorrow morning," Gareth said.

Six

"There's a woman who wants to speak with you," Rhian the receptionist said when Penny arrived at the Spa the next morning. "I told her to wait in your office and that you wouldn't be long."

"Did she give a name?" Penny asked.

"She said her name is Christina Hardwick."

A woman with shoulder-length faded blonde hair turned an eager but somewhat apprehensive face toward the door as Penny opened it.

"Hello," said Penny. "I'm Penny Brannigan. Sorry I wasn't here when you arrived. Mrs. Hardwick, is it?"

"Yes, that's right," said the woman, standing up and holding out her hand. "No need for you to apologize. I should have telephoned and asked for an appointment." She was in her late forties, wearing fashionably cut black jeans that suited her trim figure, topped with a floral patterned jacket featuring large white daisies and pink peonies on a black background. Under it she wore a low-cut black T-shirt, revealing tanned cleavage that was showing signs of crepiness.

Penny set her bag down, and pulled out her chair. "How can I help you?"

"I'll come right to the point. I want you to find out who killed my husband."

"Your husband would be John Hardwick, am I right?"

"Yes. I heard you were the one who found the body and a friend recommended I speak to you. She gets her hair done here at the Spa and said you'd been involved in solving a mystery or two." Mrs. Hardwick clasped her hands and folded them in her lap. "Look, may I be honest? I'm not sure I trust the police. There's a woman who's apparently in charge and whilst I'm sure she's very competent, she just seems a bit . . ."

"Young?" said Penny, knowing that her visitor was referring to Bethan Morgan.

"Well, I was thinking more inexperienced. I'm not confident she's up to the job. And I want whoever killed my John caught and brought to justice."

"Well, first of all, let me say how sorry I am for your loss," said Penny. "But why do you say he was killed? Did the police tell you that your husband was murdered?"

"Well, no, not in so many words. But I'm sure of it, despite the postmortem findings."

"You've been told the postmortem results?"

"Yes, that policewoman rang me about an hour ago."

"And?" prompted Penny.

Mrs. Hardwick sighed and in a voice almost dry with irritation, said, "It was inconclusive. So far. They still have toxicology tests to run and all that. But my husband didn't take drugs, so nothing's going to show up there."

Penny thought for a moment. "Mrs. Hardwick, I'm not sure what I can do for you. I've told the police everything I know. I didn't see anything. I just happened to be the one who . . ."

Christina stood up. "Well, I must say I was hoping for a bit more support from you. I do feel very let down." She was taller than Penny, and her unsmiling face was drawn and lined. "Still, if there's nothing you can do, well, I'm sorry for taking up your time."

"Mrs. Hardwick, I didn't mean it that way. Sorry I didn't make myself clear. I would like to help, if I can, it's just that I don't really think you've given the police enough time to even get their investigation started. They were waiting on the results of the postmortem so they'd know what they were dealing with. But as long as your husband's death is classified as unexplained, I believe the case remains open. It's early days as these things go, and besides that, I wouldn't want you to get your hopes up that I can do something that they can't. But please, sit down and let's talk about this. How about I get us a coffee? Or would you prefer tea?"

The woman sank back into her chair. "A cup of coffee would be brilliant, thank you. My nerves are a bit frayed, as you can imagine. And please, call me Christina."

"Right." Reluctant to leave Christina alone in case she changed her mind and decided to leave, Penny picked up her phone and asked Rhian to bring two coffees. She then returned to sit beside her visitor.

"There's a bit more to it than what I've told you," said

45

Christina Hardwick. "I do want you to find out who killed my husband, but I want you to tell just me. Not the police. I would expect this to be in the strictest confidence. Whatever you find out is just between you and me. I would then determine what to do with that information. Which may or not mean the police—but if anyone goes to the police, it will be me."

"That doesn't make any sense to me, Mrs. Hardwick," Penny said. "Christina," she corrected herself. "If I were to find out that your husband was in fact killed and who killed him, surely you would want that person brought to justice and the way to do that is through the police."

Instead of replying, Christina changed the subject. "I'm prepared to pay you very well."

Penny did not hesitate. "Mrs. Hardwick, I'm not a private detective, if that's what you're thinking, and I couldn't possibly charge a fee."

"I know you're not a proper detective, but as I said someone told me you've solved mysteries before and I'm hoping you can help me."

"May I ask who recommended me to you?"

"I'd rather not say. Just a friend."

"Well, let's just have a little chat so I can get a better idea of where things stand. Let me begin by asking you a question that I expect the police have already asked you, and if they haven't, they probably will, but can you think of anyone who would have wanted to harm your husband?"

"No, I can't," Christina replied. "He was the sweetest man you'd ever want to meet. He'd help out anybody, in any situation. Always put others before himself. Although . . ." she paused when the door opened and Rhian appeared with two coffees on a tray. Penny smiled her thanks as Rhian set it down on the desk, and then left, closing the door quietly behind her.

"You were saying?" Penny said as she handed Christina a cup.

"John wasn't without his faults, of course. He was a perfectionist and demanded as much of others as he did of himself, but he was absolutely brilliant in his work and sometimes he would get a bit impatient when others didn't see things the way he did or when their work didn't meet his standards." She took a sip of coffee and shot Penny a glance from under severely plucked eyebrows. "To be fair, I think people were jealous of his success."

"Can you tell me about that success?" Penny asked.

"Well, he'd held positions on royal estates."

"What did he do, exactly?"

"It was to do with managing the woodlands and forests. Outdoor work. He wasn't one for a desk job. He never talked much about it but what he didn't know about trees wasn't worth knowing."

"I see. And what was he doing with the Gwrych volunteers? Had they recruited him?"

"No, I don't think so," Christina said, drawing out the words. "I think he just wanted a project to work on, something in his old line of work to get him out of the house, and when he read that little article in the paper about the garden restoration work going on up there, he thought they could use his expertise."

Of course they could, thought Penny. "So he offered to help. How long ago was this? In other words, how long had he been working up at the site?"

"Oh, not long. A few weeks maybe. Six or seven weeks, I'd say."

So that fits with what Mark said, Penny thought. "And did he have any run-ins with anyone, that you know of?"

"No, of course not." She shrugged. "Well, not that he mentioned to me."

"And would he have told you?" Penny asked.

"Oh, I'm sure he would have. We always discussed the day's events over dinner."

"So you can't think of anyone who would want to harm him?"

"No, I can't."

"Could he have been in possession of something that someone else wanted?"

"Not that I'm aware of."

"Well, then, if no one wished him harm, and no one wanted something he had, we seem to be coming up short on motive. What reason do you have to think someone killed him?"

"Because there's something unnatural about his death. He'd been to the doctor and she couldn't find anything wrong with him and to just die like that." Her eyes brimmed with unshed tears and she swiped at them with her fingers. Penny held out a box of tissues. They made a soft, plucking sound as Christina pulled a couple from the box and the time it took her to do that gave each of them a moment to consider where the conversation was going.

"Well, let's leave all that to one side for the moment," said Penny. "Can you tell me more about what he was like? I'm trying to get a picture of him in my mind."

"Well, he was smart. Or did I say that already? He went to the pub every Monday for quiz night and the other teams were always trying to recruit him. He knew so much on just about any topic—history, music, culture, literature, geography—you name it. He was widely read."

"And did you have any children?"

"No, we didn't. I'm his second wife and he has a son from his first marriage. But his first wife turned the boy against John and we rarely saw him. Lately, though, she's been more open to John spending time with the lad and they were seeing more of each other. In fact, the two of them were working together up at the castle, John and his son. John really enjoyed that and that may be one of the reasons he wanted to volunteer up there. I'm not sure which came first—his first wife told him the boy was there so he volunteered, or he volunteered and discovered the boy was working there. In any event, as I said, he and his son were enjoying working together at the castle."

"I see. I'm glad to hear it."

Christina Hardwick shrugged. "How the lad is going to take all this doesn't bear thinking about. John's first marriage wasn't happy. She was an absolute witch, if you get my meaning. Of course, they were both young at the time."

"And your marriage?" Penny asked. "Was everything all right there?"

"Why on earth would you ask that?" she demanded. "What's that got to do with the murder of my husband?" She stood up. "Look, I really don't think this is going anywhere, so I'm sorry to have taken up your time. I really thought you could help me. But apparently not. Thank you anyway."

And with that, she brushed lightly past Penny, opened the door, and slipped into the hallway. Penny instinctively took a few steps after her. Christina stopped and turned round. She pulled a crumpled piece of paper out of her handbag and scribbled on it.

"If you change your mind," Christina said, holding out the paper, "ring me."

Penny watched as she turned the corner that led past the reception desk and out the front door. Unsure what to do next, she entered Victoria's office.

"What's the matter?" Victoria said, looking up from her computer. "Has something happened? Are you all right? You look, I don't know, upset?"

"I am, a little," admitted Penny. "Well, no, not upset. Just a bit puzzled. The wife, widow I guess I should say, of the man I found up at Gwrych Castle came to see me. Says she thinks there's something suspicious about the death of her husband. More than suspicious, actually. She thinks he was murdered."

"And I hope you told her that if he was, that's what the police are for and they'd be more than happy to look into it?"

"I did, yes. But she doesn't seem convinced they're up to the job. She said a friend of hers told her I'd been involved in solving a few murders and she wanted me to investigate her husband's death for her. Anyway, I asked her a few questions and when I asked her if everything was all right in her marriage, she got very shirty and stormed out. I didn't think it was an especially invasive question, under the circumstances."

"Why did you ask her that? If she'd been involved in the death of her husband, she'd hardly have come to you asking you to look into it, would she?"

Penny avoided her gaze. "I don't know why I asked her that, really. Probably because I don't know what I'm doing. I'm completely in the dark here." She dropped into the chair in front of Victoria's desk. "There's nothing at all to go on. Although she did say the postmortem didn't reveal the cause of death. So that's no help."

Victoria smiled. "And you asked all the questions, did you?" Penny nodded. "Did she ask you any?"

Penny shook her head. "No. What are you getting at?"

"Well, it seems to me that if I had a chance to speak to the person who found the body of someone I loved, or at least my husband, I would want to know everything about what happened. I'd ask if he was conscious, did he say anything, how did he look. I'd want all the details. And if he was dead, I suppose I'd be looking for reassurance that he didn't suffer. Don't you think it's odd that she didn't ask you any questions like that? Or how you came to find the body?"

"You know, you're right. I think I probably would have done that, too."

"And then when you asked about the state of her marriage and she didn't like that question, maybe it's because you hit a sensitive nerve."

"She spoke of him in the most glowing terms. How wonderful he was. How much everyone admired him. Wanted him on the pub quiz team. Quite the paragon. Sounded too good to be true."

"Yes, but did she say what she thought about him? Did she seem heartbroken? Bereaved?"

"No, not really. I think the word to describe her is . . ." Penny mulled that over for a moment. "Determined. She was determined to get her own way that I should help find out who killed her husband. But the strange thing is, she said if I did discover anything I wasn't to go to the police with it. I was to tell only her."

"Well, then."

"Well then, what?"

Victoria raised and lowered her shoulders in a small shrug of resignation. "Well, it's up to you to decide what to do, I suppose, but the whole thing sounds a bit dodgy to me."

"I guess I'll leave it alone," said Penny. "The way she left, not exactly storming out, but unpleasant enough, sent a pretty good message that her business with me was over."

Victoria turned away slightly, placed her hands on her computer keyboard, and then pulled them back into her lap. She directed a level gaze at Penny.

"Or maybe it isn't," she said. "Over."

"Now what do you mean?"

"Well, two things about this encounter bother me. First, this Mrs. Hardwick was so vague about coming to you. What was it she said? That 'a friend' had recommended you? Did you ask what friend?"

"Yes," said Penny. "She preferred not to say. Only that it was someone who gets her hair done here at the Spa, so that could mean just about anybody. She seemed so on edge that I didn't want to push her and yet apparently that's exactly what I did do."

"Well, let's leave that aside for the moment." Victoria leaned forward. "Here's what I think is a bit odd. Why come to you now? The police investigation is still only a couple of days old. I can understand why she might want to bring in someone else if the police investigation had dragged on for months with no result, but that's not the case. So why now? Why involve you so soon?"

"I wondered about that, too," said Penny. "She said she was sure her husband was killed. What's she up to?"

"Well, talk it over with Gareth. He'll know what to do."

Seven

It all seems very fishy. Especially the bit where if I do find out who killed John Hardwick I'm to tell only her who the culprit is and not the police. If he was killed, that is. And if I agree to take it on, she wants the whole thing kept confidential," Penny said to Gareth as he walked her home that evening.

They had decided to walk the long way to Penny's cottage and were almost halfway across the narrow seventeenth-century, three-arched bridge that spanned the River Conwy when the local bus turned on to it. They scuttled to safety in one of the small spaces where the stone bridge widened slightly, and flattened themselves against the well-worn stones as the bus rumbled past. The bridge had been built to accommodate pedestrians, people on horseback, or perhaps a horse-drawn cart, and Penny feared for the integrity of the beautiful structure every time a bus rumbled over it. She wished another bridge could be built farther along the river to handle modern vehicles, leaving this one to foot traffic, fulfilling the purpose for which it was designed centuries ago.

When the bridge was clear, they remained where they were, admiring the sparkling river flowing beneath them on its way to the sea. "There's definitely something odd about that," Gareth agreed. "Christina Hardwick asking you to find the killer and tell only her and that everything must be done in confidence. It's either dangerous or daft. I'm not sure which. I wonder what reason she could have for asking you to do that."

"Do you think I should mention it to Bethan?" Penny asked.

"You could, I suppose," Gareth said slowly. "Although it might be a bit difficult. 'Oh, by way, Bethan, Mrs. Hardwick's asked me to look into the death of her husband because she doesn't think you lot are up to the job.'"

Penny laughed. "Well, the way she stormed out of my office, there's nothing for me to do anyway. I'd like to forget about all that for a bit. What did you get up to today?"

"I drove into Llandudno, played nine holes of golf, did some laundry while I checked up on the house, and pulled a few weeds. And then I picked up a few things. Brought something back that I want to show you."

"Oh, where is it?"

"In my car."

While Penny slid the key into her front door and opened it, Gareth unlocked the boot of his car. He joined Penny in her sitting room carrying an old-fashioned brown leather suitcase, with brass fittings, including the locks and corners.

"Whose is that?" Penny asked. "It looks old."

"It is old," Gareth said, setting it down. "My mother packed it after my grandmother died. I've only really ever glanced in it, but all this business at Gwrych got me thinking about her. These are her things and I thought maybe you'd like to go through them with me."

"So the things in here belonged to your grandmother, Annie Evans. Wow, we have to do this right. I'm just going to pour myself a glass of wine, and then we'll open the suitcase, shall we?"

She returned a few minutes later with a glass of wine in one hand and a soft cloth in the other. She handed the cloth to Gareth, who gently wiped the dust off the top and sides of the suitcase. Penny took a sip of wine and held up the glass.

He shook his head. "No, I'll have something later, maybe." He turned the case on its side and placed his hands on the locks. "Ready?" On her nod he clicked both locks and gently swung the lid open. Penny got down on her knees beside him and they peered at the contents.

On top lay several sheets of white tissue paper. Gareth lifted the paper, revealing a hand-stitched piece of needlework about the size of a small hand towel. He lifted out the needlework and tissue paper and handed them to Penny, who arranged them gently on the floor, the needlework resting on top of the tissue paper.

"I think it's called a sampler," said Penny. "It was sometimes used as an example of a young woman's stitching skills or to record stitch samples for teaching purposes. Or maybe it's just needlework, but anyway, this is absolutely beautiful. I wonder if there's a date on it." Worked in counted stitches in wool and silk against a green background on a double canvas, the colours of the piece were as bright as the day it was made. Examining it more closely, Penny let out a little gasp on recognition. "Oh, you're going to have to show this to Mark Baker," she said.

Enclosed in a decorative border of pink roses and ivy, the various designs on the needlework all appeared related to Gwrych Castle. Gareth pointed to a tree with what looked like large spikes coming out of the trunk. "Look, there's even a monkey puzzle tree." He moved his finger. "And here's one of the towers."

"And the main gates," added Penny.

The creator of the work had positioned the most striking, eye-catching element at its heart. "Wow. Look at that," Penny said, pointing to the bright red splash running up the centre. "It looks like the grand staircase with its red carpet. I read about that online." After admiring the needlepoint canvas for a few more moments, Penny rolled it in the layers of tissue paper. "We'll have to take very good care of this," she remarked as Gareth lifted out a dark item of clothing. He set it to one side, then pulled out a blue-and-silver tin biscuit box with images of King George V and Queen Mary on the top and SILVER JUBILEE 1910–1935 embossed on the side.

"What are you betting these are photographs?" Gareth asked. "Let's make ourselves more comfortable while we look at them." Holding the box, he stood up and pulled Penny to her feet. They sat beside each other on the sofa and Gareth removed the lid revealing piles of pictures. One by one he sorted through them, looking at the image, turning it over to see if anything was written on the back, then handing it to Penny. When he came to a photo of a small boy in short trousers holding the hands of a man and a woman, he chuckled as he handed it to Penny.

"Here you go," he said.

"You?" she said. He nodded and turned to the next photograph, sifting through one woman's lifetime of memories captured in black and white with details sometimes recorded on the reverse in spidery handwriting. As the photos receded in time, the 1950s fading into the Second World War, the dresses becoming longer, hats becoming smaller, once again Gwrych Castle came into view. Gareth separated these photos from the others. Exterior views of the castle with manicured gardens, much smaller trees, and a fresh, cared-for look. But of more interest were the photos of unsmiling people in awkward poses, offering incidental glimpses into rooms frozen in time. Tall ferns in massive jardineres set against dark oak paneling in the grand hall gave the room an Edwardian feel while armour and tapestries contributed to a medieval look. "Blimey," said Gareth, pointing at the centre of a black-and-white image. "Look at the size of that fireplace. You could roast an ox in it." He set the photo in the Gwrych pile.

"Mark will certainly want copies of these for his archives," he said, reaching for the next one.

"You know he will," said Penny.

"But he's not getting the embroidery."

"Of course not. Speaking of which," said Penny, "I should have a word with Alwynne at the museum about how best to preserve it. I'm sure she'll say continue to keep it out of the sunlight, and might suggest it be stored in acid-free paper."

"Good idea," said Gareth, handing Penny the next photo.

"Oh, the marble staircase," she said, taking it from him and tilting it toward the light. "Just like on the tapestry. I saw colour photos of it online and it's interesting that even back then a red carpet was recognized as something special. We think of that as a modern concept used for award shows and so on, but it isn't."

They finished looking at the photos and Gareth replaced them in the biscuit tin.

"If you'd like to stay for dinner, why don't you get things started while I let Mark know about the photos?" Penny suggested. A few minutes later she joined him in the kitchen and as he handed her a couple of potatoes to peel she said, "He couldn't wait to see what you've got. He's just on his way back from Bangor and he's coming over after dinner."

Eight

Mark held up his empty hands.

"Sorry. The second I saw you I realized I forgot to bring you a copy of the book. I'll put a copy in the car so I have one with me the next time I see you."

"Well, I'll hold you to that," Penny said, leading him into her sitting room. "I'd offer you a cup of coffee, but let's wait until you're finished with the photos. We don't want to risk a spill."

Mark took a seat at the table with Gareth and the two began poring over the photographs, with Mark capturing each image on his mobile phone.

"This is a real treasure trove," he said. "I'm stunned. Thrilled, but stunned. Makes me wonder how many more photographs are out there, hidden in trunks and suitcases."

He picked up the photo of the marble staircase. "Here's the same view," he said, showing them an image on his phone. "This is the best colour photo of it, to my knowledge."

"Tell us about it," said Gareth.

"Yes," said Penny, folding her arms on the table and leaning on them, "please do. As I haven't been able to read about it in that book I'm so desperate to get my hands on. What was it called, again? Something like *The Rise and Fall of Gwrych Castle,* maybe?"

Mark threw her a resigned, amused look, then settled back into his chair and sighed as Gareth packed up the photographs. "When you mention Gwrych to people who live in the area, or to anybody who saw it before the 1990s, inevitably it's the staircase they remember best. Without a doubt, the marble staircase was the building's most prominent and best known feature. It was installed in 1914 as part of a major refurbishment and was designed by the architect Detmar Blow, who did a lot of work for the British aristocracy.

"The staircase was amazing—fifty-two marble steps, divided into two landings, that led straight up. No turns or twists. Just a beautiful stairway with a stunning red carpet—Axminster, of course—running down the middle. The marble in the stairs had purple and black striations and there was a green marble dado running up the side. All of the finest Italian marble. It just seemed to stretch on forever, ending in a memorial stained glass window."

"I wish I could have seen it," said Penny. "It must have been spectacular."

"It was," agreed Mark. "I saw it, although I'm not sure

I remember it. My parents have a picture of me as a little boy sitting on it. By the time I was old enough to take an interest in the buildings and try do something about the terrible condition they were in, the marble was gone, but the basic underlying structure for the stairs was still there. Now, of course, even that's gone."

"Now that you mention it, I've just remembered that I saw it, too," said Gareth. "The staircase. When the castle buildings were open to visitors, everyone made a point of seeing it. In fact, one day my friends and I played on it until our parents told us to stop. There were statues holding lamps and a great chandelier over it and metal railings on the landings that overlooked it. No wonder it's always referred to as a grand staircase. It was famous. And would I be right, Mark, that most of the fixtures and fittings were stolen in the 1990s?"

"That's correct. By new age travellers, we think. But you can't blame them, really. The owners of the property at that time had no security in place, so it was an open invitation for squatters, thieves, and the like to come in and help themselves. So they did. Every room was thoroughly picked over and stripped of everything that might conceivably have value. And what wasn't stolen and sold on was vandalized or people took bits away for souvenirs."

He turned to Penny. "I write about it in my book. You'll see. I'm really sorry I haven't been able to get that copy to you. But I will."

"It's hard to think of a staircase being stolen," said Penny, "but it's not as unusual as you might think. Do you know what the most valuable object ever stolen was?"

"No," said Gareth. "I'd guess a painting? A Rembrandt? An old master like that?"

"You'd think that," said Penny, "but it wasn't. It was a room."

"Oooh," said Mark as the answer dawned on him. "The Amber Room stolen by the Nazis from the Catherine Palace in Saint Petersburg during the Second World War."

"That's right," said Penny. "An entire room crafted entirely of amber, gold, mirrors, and precious stones dismantled, packed in crates, and put on a train to Germany. Its last known whereabouts was the castle in Königsberg. But the castle was bombed during the last days of the war and no one knows what happened to the Amber Room."

"It's thought to be still in boxes, stowed down a mine or in some old bunker," said Mark, "but as you say, no one really knows."

"So if the Nazis could steal an entire room, it's more than possible the marble staircase was stolen. What do you think happened to it?" Gareth asked Mark.

"I expect the marble was sold to a building supply company that specializes in reclaimed architectural features and it was then installed in somebody's property. I'm sure it still exists somewhere. And the same goes for the roofing slates, the clock from the stable yard, and all the other elements that were stolen. They're out there."

"There's something else we wanted to show you before I get you that coffee," Penny said, laying the needlework on the table.

Mark gasped, then raised a hand to his mouth. "Wow." He leaned forward to examine it. "It's beautiful." He turned to Gareth. "Would this be your grandmother's work?"

"I assume so," said Gareth. "It was in with her things."

"May I photograph it?" Mark asked.

"Of course." Gareth positioned the cloth on the table and stepped out of Mark's light. "Have you heard anything more from the police?" he asked as Mark snapped a few photographs.

"Not since you were on site," he replied. "The police-woman was there to tell us that they'd wrapped up what they needed to do and we could take down the tape from around the stables and start working there again. But there is something I thought I should mention." He tucked his phone in his pocket as he straightened up. Penny re-moved the needlework from the table, and placed a cup of coffee on the table in front of him. He gave her a quick nod of thanks.

"We had a new volunteer join us a few days before Hardwick died. She just started hanging around, asking a lot of questions, and then finally decided not to get involved with our project. According to one of the people I talked to, she wasn't much of a worker. Didn't do as she was asked, didn't stick with the team. Wandered off, looking around on her own. It was almost as if she was using the volunteer-ing as an opportunity to get access to the site, if you know what I mean."

Gareth nodded. "Go on."

"Well, that's all there is to it, really."

"Is she still there?"

"No, apparently she stopped showing up."

"Did you see her yourself?"

"No. Just going by what I was told. I don't have much to do with the ground clearance operations or building restoration. I look after grant applications, fund-raising, and publicity to keep the project alive."

"You wouldn't happen to know this new volunteer's name, by any chance, would you? Do you screen your volunteers? Ask for references, that sort of thing?"

Mark took a sip of coffee. "Not really. We just have them fill out a form so we can contact them if we have to. They have to sign a waiver—you know, in case of injury. And we ask for the name of someone in case of an accident. The work isn't dangerous, or it shouldn't be, but just to be on the safe side.

"The thing is, ground clearance is hard, boring work, and we're lucky to get a few guys willing to help out. The whole estate is in desperate need of help, as you know, and we're starting with the grounds. We get a better turn out of volunteers on the weekend, of course, because most people are at work during the day. It's mostly men but we get a few women who don't mind getting their hands dirty. That's why this volunteer seemed a bit unusual."

"Speaking of hands, do you provide equipment, like work gloves?"

"We have some they can borrow, but most people bring their own."

Gareth remained silent while his eyes flickered in Penny's direction. Then he turned back to Mark. "Your volunteers. Do they just show up and offer to help or do they let you know they're interested and you give them a date and time to start?"

"Well, you'd probably have to ask Ifor Jones that question but I think people just show up. There's somebody there most days. The police told us not to post the hours we're there on our Web site."

"Quite right," agreed Gareth.

"Because . . ." said Penny.

Gareth and Mark exchanged a quick glance and at the go-ahead nod from Gareth, Mark said, "Because by telling people when we're there, we're also telling them when we're not there and that leaves us open to vandals. God knows we have enough problems with that as it is."

"I've never understood what possible pleasure someone could get out of throwing a rock through a window or spray-painting a wall," said Gareth, "and I've seen a lot of it. Vandalism just seems like the stupidest, most mindless of crimes. Usually people commit crimes for gain, but I've never understood what they gain by vandalism."

"It's a way of leaving something of yourself behind, I suppose," said Mark. "For people who have nothing good to offer." He set down his coffee cup and stood up, signaling he was on his way. "Well, I'm meeting up with someone so I'd best be off. But thank you so much for showing me the photographs and needlework. They're very special."

When Mark had left, Gareth and Penny gathered up the photos and replaced them in the suitcase. Penny admired the needlework one last time, then rolled it up gently in its tissue paper. After standing the suitcase against the wall, Gareth turned to her.

"I've been thinking about volunteering to do some work at the castle. I could use a bit of exercise."

Penny laughed. "Really? If it's gardening you're after,

you've got a perfectly good garden at home that could probably use some attention."

"Well, that's true. But what do you say we pack a picnic and head over to Gwrych in the morning? You can work on your painting and I'll lend a hand with whatever they're doing. Sounds like they're hard up for help, so they might be able to use an old fellow like me."

"I'm sure they can," said Penny. "I'll let Mark know."

"I'll head home now to get some suitable work clothes and I'll pick you up tomorrow at, what, half nine? Let's keep our ears open and see what we can learn, especially about this new volunteer."

"And what about Ifor Jones?"

"He's of interest as well. Everybody is, as long as the case remains open."

"I don't suppose Bethan would be willing to share any information with you."

"No, I don't suppose she would and I wouldn't dream of asking her. But if we come up with anything that I think she should know, of course I'll tell her."

"I hope she doesn't think you're on her patch. Or worse, that you don't trust her to do the job."

"I do trust her," he replied. "She'll get there. I just want to be ready for her if she asks for my help."

Nine

"If you'll just take a seat and complete this form," said Ifor Jones, handing Gareth a clipboard and gesturing to a plastic garden chair propped up against the shipping container, "I've got a couple of things to see to, and when I come back we'll get you started." As Ifor walked away, Gareth lifted the corner of the piece of paper he had been asked to fill out, revealing a completed volunteer form underneath. He noted the name and address and then pulled his phone out of his pocket and photographed the document.

Ifor returned with a fluorescent lime green high-visibility jacket, which he handed to Gareth, then directed him to the area where volunteers were freeing a limestone wall from the tangled tentacles of climbing ivy that had had decades to take hold.

"I'll walk up with you and introduce you," Ifor said.

"The lads have been going at this ivy for weeks and have done a brilliant job of clearing it away. They've actually revealed these walls have supporting buttresses, something we didn't know before. And with the trimming that's been done on the tree branches higher up, light is actually starting to filter through."

They reached the area at the far end of the wall, near the ice tower. Four men looked up as Gareth and Ifor approached. Three seemed to be around Gareth's age and the fourth considerably younger.

"Got a new recruit, lads," he said to the little group. "This is Gareth. He's going to be joining us today." The men muttered greetings and then all but one returned to removing the ivy and piling it near the path.

"Gareth, this is Carwyn Williams," Ifor said, introducing him to the last man. "He's the unofficial leader of this group, and he'll show you the ropes. Any questions, just ask Carwyn." The man removed a work glove and held out a rough, red hand, which Gareth shook. He found himself looking into Carwyn's weathered face, lined as if he had spent a good part of his working life outdoors, farming perhaps. A pair of bright blue eyes embedded in puffy eye bags gazed back at him, with curious, benign interest.

"So how long have you been doing this, then?" Gareth asked.

"The better part of a year," Carwyn replied, handing him a stiff brush. "Here, I'll show you how it's done. You need a light touch, mind, otherwise you'll ruin the stone work." He demonstrated how to pull the ivy off. "The roots are everywhere and if you pull too hard, you risk damaging the wall. Gently does it." As the ivy he'd removed fell to the ground, he took the brush from Gareth and swiped at the wall where the ivy had been. "The brush removes the roots, see. And if you can't get all of it, don't worry about it. Better to leave some root than ruin the mortar. It's fragile enough as it is. You make a start and I'll send someone over to help you in a few minutes."

Gareth set to work. After about fifteen minutes, when he thought he was starting to see results, he stepped back to examine his work. One of the men, the youngest one, approached him holding out a bottle of water. He was rail thin and fine featured with shoulder-length, sandy-coloured hair.

"You look thirsty," he said in a breathy, slightly high-pitched voice. "I thought you could do with a drink."

"Oh, thanks very much." Gareth accepted the bottle with a smile and unscrewed the cap.

"We can take a break whenever we like. They're not too strict," said the young man. Gareth asked him his name.

"Lane."

"Good to meet you, Lane." Gareth took a sip of water and tipped his head in the vague direction of the other volunteers, working a little way farther down the wall. "You're young to be working here with the rest of us old retired types."

"If you're asking why I don't have a regular job to go to, I'm between proper jobs at the minute, so Mum suggested I might put in some hours here. To get me out of the house, like, and give me something useful to do. Where I could make a contra . . ." he stumbled over the word. "Do something useful."

"Well good for you," said Gareth. "And thank you for

the water. Now, I suppose I'd better . . ." he gestured at the wall.

"I can help you," said Lane. "I know how to do this."

They fell into a companionable rhythm, as Gareth removed the plant growth and Lane followed along after him, brushing away the newly exposed roots. "And do you enjoy it?" Gareth asked. "Working here?"

"Oh, yes. I like being outdoors on such a beautiful day. Don't like it in the rain, though. This place is spooky in the rain."

"Yes," agreed Gareth. "I guess it would be." Something in the earnestness of the young man's voice made him take a closer look. Gareth estimated he was in his mid-twenties. He wore a faded blue T-shirt with an image of palm trees and the neon Hotel California script emblazoned across it. His blue jeans hung loosely on his hips. His dark brown eyes searched Gareth's face and then darted round the site, coming to rest on the little group of men ahead of them.

"Are you an Eagles fan?" Gareth asked him.

"Huh?"

"Your shirt. Hotel California. Eagles. The rock band. Fan, are you?"

Lane swiped at his chest with dusty fingers and raised a shoulder a fraction. "It's something to wear, I guess. I don't take much notice. Are you going to have lunch soon?" he asked without meeting Gareth's eyes.

"Well, I don't know. I really only just got started. I guess we'll have lunch when the others do, won't we?"

"I could talk to Carwyn and ask him what time we're going to lunch. I'm hungry."

"Maybe you could go for lunch now, then." Lane studied Gareth's work boots. "What is it, Lane? Is something bothering you?"

"I forgot my lunch," Lane said. "I remembered to bring the water, but forgot my lunch."

"You mean the water was all you had and you gave it to me?"

Lane nodded. "You looked thirsty. I thought you needed it more than I did."

"Oh, if I'd known that I never would have . . . I thought there were bottles stashed away for the volunteers and you were giving me one of those. But listen, never mind about forgetting your lunch. That's not a problem. Not a problem at all. I'm here with my friend and we brought a picnic and she always packs too much, so there'll be lots to share. What kind of sandwich do you like? Do you like ham and tomato?"

Lane's face lit up. "It's my favourite."

"Good. Because I'm pretty sure that's what we've got for lunch. I'll let Carwyn know we're going to have an early lunch, then, shall I?"

"And I'd like an apple, too, if you've got one going spare."

With Lane slouching along behind him, Gareth made his way along the main terrace to the garden area at the other end of the property where Penny was sketching. She smiled when the two approached her, and nodded when Gareth explained they would be sharing their picnic.

"Lane's hungry now so we arranged to take an early lunch," he said.

73

"Perfect," said Penny. "I'm getting hungry myself." She handed each of them a moist towelette to wipe their hands, then passed around sandwiches, cheese, and biscuits from the cooler. She poured three glasses of water from a large bottle.

"This is good," Lane said, holding up his sandwich. "My mum, she makes good sandwiches, too, but I forgot to bring them today. They'll be at home in the fridge. Maybe I'll eat them for my tea." Penny held out a plastic container filled with celery and carrots. "I know you," Lane said as he chose a piece of celery. "I've seen you before." He bit the end off it, and munched noisily.

"You do?" said Penny. "I'm sorry, if we've met before I don't remember it."

"Right here you were," said Lane. "Well, not right here. Not on this very spot. Over there, you were." He gestured toward the Melon House. "We didn't meet but I saw you. You were there, painting, like you are today. You were here the day that bad thing happened." He held a hand up to the side of his head and squeezed his eyes shut. "Very bad thing."

Ten

What bad thing do you mean?" Gareth asked gently. "When what bad thing happened?" Lane did not reply but opened his eyes and stared at the ground. "Do you mean when the body of that man was found? Is that what you mean, Lane? Were you here that day?" Lane nodded and Penny and Gareth exchanged worried looks.

"Are you all right?" Penny asked. When Lane did not reply, she asked him again.

"Yeah, I'm fine." He looked round, and then brightened. "Have we got any biscuits?"

"We do," said Penny, holding out a packet. "Chocolate digestives."

"They're my favourite," said Lane, helping himself to two. He turned to Gareth. "If you want, we can go to the shed where we sign in and out. We can make tea there. There's a kettle. If you want tea with your biscuit."

"I don't think I'll have any tea just now, thanks. But you go if you want to."

"No, I'll stay here with you. I like it better here with you." He dropped the biscuits on his plate. "There's no fighting. They were fighting, and I didn't like that." He covered his ears with his hands.

"Was somebody fighting this morning?" Gareth asked. Lane shook his head as he slowly lowered his hands. Gareth placed a reassuring hand on Lane's arm. "Do you want to tell me who was fighting?"

"No, not this morning," he said with a tinge of impatience as if Gareth should know what he was referring to. "The other day. They were shouting. I tried to get away from it. It reminded me of when I was little and Mum and Dad used to fight. I don't like it."

"The other day? Do you mean the day the . . ." he hesitated, "the day the bad thing happened here?" Lane nodded as he took a bite of his biscuit. "And have you spoken to anyone about what happened?" Gareth asked quietly.

"Not really," said Lane. "No, I guess not."

"Did the police ask you any questions about what you heard?"

"No, they didn't talk to me. I took the bus home, like I always do. I've got my bus pass. I can go anywhere I like with it."

"I take the bus most places, too," said Penny. "Did you have enough to eat, Lane? Couple more biscuits here if you'd like them." She held out the remains of the red packet.

"You could save them for later, to have with a cup of tea. Just don't keep them in the pocket of your jeans. They'll get broken and the chocolate will melt and it'll be messy." He accepted her offering, folded the paper wrapping tightly round the remaining biscuits and tucked them in the pocket of his jacket, while Penny replaced the remains of the picnic in the cooler.

"Well," said Gareth. "Back to work, then?" He scanned the grounds, looking for the other volunteers. "Do we normally go back to what we were doing for the afternoon or are we reassigned to another project?"

"It depends," said Lane. "But I'm not staying for the afternoon. I've got a doctor's appointment so I'm going to leave now. You can talk to Carwyn or Ifor and see what they need you to do this afternoon."

"I'll do that," said Gareth. "Well, thank you for showing me the ropes."

"No problem," said Lane, looking at his shoes.

"Look," said Gareth, "if you'd like me to drive to your appointment, I'd be happy to."

"No, I told you. I've got my bus pass. I like to get around on my own. I listen to my music on the bus. See you." He sloped off down the bank toward the road that led to the castle gates and the bus stop beyond.

"What do you make of that?" asked Penny, as Lane's figure diminished.

"I'm pretty sure he saw or heard something, and it's traumatized him," Gareth replied as he sat down beside her on the plaid rug. "I don't have a good feeling about this."

"Something he said . . . that he knew me. That got me

thinking. I think he's right. I'm pretty sure I've seen him before, but I can't remember where," Penny responded.

Evelyn Lloyd checked her watch as the bus approached the Castle Gates stop. Another half hour at least before they'd be home and she was desperate for a cup of tea. She glanced at Florence Semble in the aisle seat beside her, nose buried in her library book. Perhaps sensing Mrs. Lloyd's eyes upon her, Florence looked up, leaned slightly forward, and glanced out the window to get her bearings, returned to her novel and turned the page. When the bus stopped and the doors opened a young man got on, placed his pass on the electronic card reader and then scanned the bus looking for an empty seat. He settled in the window seat directly in front of Mrs. Lloyd and positioned a pair of white in-ear headphones. A moment later the faintly tinny sound of music rose from his ears to hers. Mrs. Lloyd sighed. Just one more annoyance in a long day of them.

As town gave way to country, Mrs. Lloyd settled back in her seat and watched the vivid patchwork of green fields and grey stone walls flash by. Out here in the country, the stops were fewer and the bus made good time. At the reassuring thought that she was getting closer to her cup of tea, she perked up. And then a small sound coming from the seat in front of her caught her attention. It took her a moment to realize that the young man wearing the ear phones was sniffling and wiping his eyes with the back of his hand. She nudged Florence and tipped her head in his direction. Florence shot her a questioning look. 'Should we do something?' it asked. Mrs. Lloyd opened her handbag and pulled out a packet of tissues. Raising an eyebrow at Florence she handed it to her. Florence reached round and offered it to the young man. He took it, pulled out a tissue, and blew his nose noisily. He turned and tried to give the packet back to her but she shook her head.

"You keep it," she said, with a soft, reassuring smile. She sat back in her seat, nodded at Mrs. Lloyd, and tried to resume her reading. But after seeming to have read the same paragraph several times, she closed the book and tucked it in her bag. For the rest of the journey Florence and Mrs. Lloyd stared silently out the window.

As the bus pulled into Llanelen, they prepared to alight. Mrs. Lloyd exchanged a few words with the driver while Florence gathered up their shopping bags from the low-railed luggage compartment at the front of the bus. While she was doing that, the young man in the Eagles T-shirt squeezed past her, with a polite, "Excuse me," alighted from the bus, and loped off toward the town square.

When they were standing on the pavement, Florence handed Mrs. Lloyd a bag of groceries for each hand. As they set off toward the home they shared on Rosemary Lane Mrs. Lloyd glanced over her shoulder.

"What a day this has been, Florence," she remarked a few minutes later as she pushed open their black wrought-iron gate. "That poor lad. Whatever upset him, I wonder." Florence followed her up the path, then set down her bags while she fished her house key out of her handbag. "Perhaps his girlfriend gave him his walking papers," said Florence as she opened the door and stood to one side so Mrs. Lloyd could enter.

"I thought I was desperate for a cup of tea, but I realize

now it's a glass of sherry I fancy," she said as she kicked off her shoes and entered the sitting room. "May I pour one for you, Florence?"

"Yes, please," came the response from the kitchen. "I'll be with you as soon as I've put the shopping away."

Eleven

"Well, what have you got on today?" Mrs. Lloyd asked the next morning, studying Florence over the rim of her cup as she sipped the last of her coffee.

"Not much. I thought I'd do some tidying up in my bedroom and then walk into town, change my library books, and maybe have a coffee in the café with Jean. Is there anything you need whilst I'm out?"

"No, you're all right," said Mrs. Lloyd, pushing in her chair and carrying her breakfast dishes through to the kitchen. She set them in the sink and poured warm water from the kettle over them just as Florence entered and switched on the radio. The sounds of an old Dusty Springfield song filled the sunny kitchen. Mrs. Lloyd started singing along and Florence joined in.

"They don't make songs like they used to, do they?" commented Mrs. Lloyd as the music ended.

"They certainly don't," agreed Florence, turning on the tap to start the washing up. "How could anyone possibly sing along to that rap music or whatever it's called? Let alone dance." Before Mrs. Lloyd could respond, the announcer's voice caught their attention. "North Wales police are appealing for help in finding a missing man from Llanelen." The two women looked at each other and Florence turned off the water. "Lane Hardwick, aged twenty-four, was last seen leaving Gwrych Castle yesterday afternoon just before one P.M. He's described as five feet, nine inches tall, with shoulder-length, sandy-brown hair and a slight build. He is believed to be wearing a blue T-shirt with an emblem on it from the American rock band the Eagles and blue jeans."

"Oh, my word, Florence! That's the lad who rode the bus with us!" Mrs. Lloyd exclaimed.

"As it is out of character for him to stay out overnight, his family is very concerned for his safety. If you have seen this young man and can help police with their inquiries, please call Detective Inspector Bethan Morgan on . . ." Florence jotted down the telephone number and checked it as the announcer repeated it.

"Here, give me that," Mrs. Lloyd said, taking the piece of paper out of Florence's hand. "I'll ring the police right now."

At North Wales police service headquarters, PC Chris Jones put the phone down, walked along the corridor to Det.

Inspector Bethan Morgan's office, and knocked. She looked up from her computer.

"Had a couple of calls about the missing lad," he said, "and they look solid." He glanced at the paper in his hand. "Our old friend Mrs. Evelyn Lloyd of Llanelen says that she saw him get on and off the number X88 bus. He seemed upset. And just before that, our old boss the former DCI Davies and Penny Brannigan, would you believe, ate lunch with him at Gwrych Castle."

Bethan groaned and then laughed. "What is it with these people always turning up in the middle of almost every investigation? Very well, you'd better bring the car around. Apparently we've got people to talk to. We'll start with Mrs. Lloyd whilst we're still fresh."

Florence opened the door to the two police officers and gestured to the sitting room on her right, saying, "You know the way by now." Mrs. Lloyd stood up as they entered.

"Well, you didn't waste any time getting here, I must say."

"We're anxious to find this young man," Bethan said. "His mother is very worried. He is developmentally challenged so naturally she's terribly concerned." She tipped her head at the constable who pulled out his notebook.

"Normally, I'd interview you separately, but in this case I think it might be more helpful if I talked to you together. I want you to tell me everything. Don't leave anything out. Don't filter your thoughts trying to decide if something's important or not. We'll decide what's relevant. Start at the beginning, please. Was he on the bus when you got on or were you on the bus and he got on?"

"We were on the bus and he got on at the Castle Gates stop, I'm pretty sure it was," said Mrs. Lloyd. "Florence was that engrossed in her book but I noticed him right away. He sat in front of us. We were in the raised seats, you know the ones that are higher, so he sat lower in front of us. He put on his music and then we noticed he seemed upset. He seemed to be crying so we offered him a pack of tissues." Bethan gave her an encouraging nod. "Which he took and then blew his nose. And he stayed on the bus all the way to the end, just like we did, and got off at the Watling Street stop here in Llanelen.

"We were concerned about him, but well, you don't like to stick your oar in, do you? And besides, he's a young man, so we wouldn't have wanted to embarrass him, over the crying. I wondered if maybe he'd had a break up with his girlfriend, but you can't really ask, can you?"

"What about you, Florence?" said Bethan. "Do you agree with everything Mrs. Lloyd just said? Is that how you remember it?"

Florence nodded vigorously. "Absolutely."

"And can you add anything?" Bethan asked.

"Well, I was pulling our carrier bags out of the luggage rack—you know the space beside the door with the rails on it where you can leave your shopping, and he brushed past me and got off the bus. He was very polite. He said, 'Excuse me.'"

"I was talking to the driver," Mrs. Lloyd chimed in. "It was his last day before retiring and I was very sorry to see him go. Always reliable and helpful, he was. He'll be missed. I've seen him on several routes. Peter Jones, his name is, if you need to speak to him."

"And did you see what direction the young man went in?" Bethan asked. "I want you to close your eyes and picture yourself back on the street. You're standing beside the bus and the lad is . . . well, you tell me. Where is he and what direction is he going?"

The two women exchanged a quick glance and then closed their eyes.

"Well, he headed off toward the town square, and we went the other way to come home," said Mrs. Lloyd, opening her eyes. "I glanced back over my shoulder just as we left and I saw him crossing the square in the direction of the bank."

"Did you see him with anybody? Did anyone meet him off the bus or approach him in the street at all?" Bethan asked.

Florence rubbed her eyes gently, as if trying to freeze the moment and fix an image. "Wait," she said, "there is something. I could be wrong, but I thought I saw him raise a hand. Like this." She lifted her hand. "Could he have been waving to someone? And if so, does that mean he spotted someone he knew?" She opened her eyes. "Sorry, that's the best I can do."

"Is there anything else you remember?" asked Bethan.

"I think that's it," said Mrs. Lloyd. "For me, anyhow."

Bethan thanked them, and after giving them her business card and telling them to ring her if they remembered anything else, no matter how trivial it may seem, she and PC Chris Jones left. When they were outside, Bethan turned to him and remarked, "I might have made a procedural error there."

"Interviewing them together?"

"Yeah."

"Oh, well, it's done now. But I'm sure you got some good information off them."

"Let's hope the DCI and Penny can fill in a few more blanks."

"Come in." Penny welcomed Det. Inspector Bethan Morgan and PC Chris Jones into her sitting room. The curtains fluttered in the light breeze wafting in from the front garden. A glass pitcher of lemonade, its sides dripping with condensation, and four glasses on a small side table greeted them.

"Oh, lovely," said Bethan. "Just what we need."

Penny poured each police officer a glass, and then sat beside Gareth on the sofa. Bethan looked from one to the other.

"I'm sure you discussed your recollections of your encounter with Lane when you heard he'd disappeared and all this became a police matter," she said. "But you know interviewing protocol," she said, giving her former boss a cool, impartial look, "so I'm going to speak to each of you separately, to make sure we get the best memories from each of you."

"Who would you like first?" he asked.

"Who do you think?" she replied.

"Me."

"Right, then. Penny, if you wouldn't mind excusing us for a few minutes."

"I'll be upstairs. Just call up when you're ready for me."

When Penny had left the room, Bethan opened her questioning by asking Gareth to tell her everything he remembered about what had happened yesterday at Gwrych. He described the details of the day in precise, neutral language.

When they were finished, Bethan excused him and called Penny downstairs. Her account wasn't as detailed as Gareth's because she had met Lane just at lunch. "And then I gave him the last two chocolate digestive biscuits, he put them in his pocket and left," she concluded. "We watched him make his way along the drive to the main gates, and presumably from there to the bus stop."

Bethan invited Gareth back into the sitting room.

"Confirming what he was wearing is helpful as his mother wasn't sure. She didn't see him leave the house in the morning. She said on one hand she was surprised he wanted to return to Gwrych Castle so soon after the discovery of the body. She said it had really upset him, as of course it would. On the other hand, she could understand his going back because he loves the place and she thought it would be a good distraction for him. She left work early to pick him up at his medical appointment, as they'd agreed, and became concerned when they told her he hadn't turned up. Which apparently, was unlike him. He's gone to appointments on his own before without any problems."

"And his phone?" Gareth asked. "Sorry. Couldn't resist asking. You just tell me if I step out of line, but old habits die hard."

"No, it's all right. He's not answering. Goes directly to voice mail. Of course we've told his mother to try not to worry too much."

"But she must be worried half to death," said Penny.

"Yes, she is. He's vulnerable. To be honest, I'm rather worried, too. When she says this is completely out of character I believe her. Still, the information we got this morning is a good start. We have him with you at the castle, then we have him positively identified alighting from the bus at the Watling Street stop and heading toward the town square. We know he was in some distress. After that . . . nothing." She turned to the constable.

"You'd better get onto the businesses surrounding the bus stop and check their CCTV footage. It would help us focus our search if we knew what direction he was headed in so we can work out where he was probably going or what he was after." She took a sip of lemonade as PC Jones left. "So let's just go over again what we know. You shared your picnic lunch with Lane at the castle and he seemed upset, a bit on edge—would that be a good way to describe him?"

"Yes, that's fair," said Gareth.

"And after he finished having lunch with you he left to catch the bus. He didn't go back to work."

"Right."

"But on the bus he was seen crying. I wonder if someone said something to him on the way out. You didn't see him talking to anyone?"

"No," said Penny. "He left right after we finished lunch and I carried on with my painting."

"And I went back to work clearing the ivy off the wall at the far end," said Gareth.

"So this volunteering at the castle. Is this your retirement project?" Bethan asked.

"Not really, I don't know how much longer I'll do it. Penny's been up there sketching, and I thought it might be interesting to join her and lend a hand for a few days."

"I'm doing a series of watercolours to be auctioned off as a fund-raiser," Penny explained. "I'm sure I mentioned it in my statement; that's why I was up there sketching when I found John Hardwick's body."

"It's just that if I can arrange it with my superiors, it occurred to me that it might be a good idea to have you," she looked at Gareth, "there with your eyes and ears open, if you know what I mean. With the discovery of the body and now the disappearance of this young man, something might be happening at the castle that we should know about."

"Are you asking me to do undercover work?"

"Yes, something like that, although maybe police informer is more like it. You wouldn't have official police powers, of course, but you'd pass on anything you learn to me."

"I don't think we need any kind of permission or arrangement. I'd do that anyway. And that reminds me. One other thing from yesterday that may or not be significant. Mark Baker mentioned a volunteer had recently turned up, but didn't do any work, just seemed to be checking the place out, hung around for a bit and then didn't come back. I spotted this on the clipboard when I was asked to complete a volunteer registration form." He showed Bethan the application form he had photographed. "I don't know, of course, if this person has any bearing on your misper, but here are her details in case you want to follow up."

"Angela Livingstone," read Bethan. She glanced from Penny to Gareth. "Does that name mean anything to either of you?" Her query was met with blank looks. "We'll keep this in mind," she said. "Can you e-mail it to me?"

"I'll do that right now."

"The missing lad, Lane, he seemed distressed when we were talking to him," Penny said. "I got the feeling he might have heard or seen something the day that Hardwick died. And you said something just now that intrigued me. You said his mother was surprised he went back up there 'so soon after.' So soon after the discovery of Hardwick, did you mean?"

Bethan nodded. "Yes, the whole thing has hit Lane particularly hard and his mother was surprised he went back there."

She looked from one blank, puzzled face to the other.

"You didn't know? John Hardwick was Lane's father."

Twelve

O h, no," said Gareth, a deep frown creasing his forehead. "I didn't know. This changes everything. Let me help, Bethan," he implored. "The boy could be in real danger and I speak from experience when I tell you that you don't want to look back on this and think, 'We should have done more,' or 'We could have saved him.' You know how critical the first twenty-four hours are. Let me help," he repeated. When she didn't reply, he pressed on. "Have you searched his room?" She nodded. "And?"

"I remembered what you taught me. That nothing is random. That everything he has in his room is connected to something or someone and it's there for a reason. But I didn't see anything out of the ordinary. Although the room seemed more suited for a teenager than a young man. The usual stuff on the walls, a bit messy, single bed—that sort of thing."

"And was his mother able to give you a list of his friends? Someone he might be staying with?"

"No. She said he doesn't have any friends. He was bullied at school, apparently, and spends most of his time alone. Or with a much younger boy."

Penny tucked her hair behind her ears and leaned forward, her hands resting on her knees.

"When you searched his room, did you notice a library card?" she asked.

"No," Bethan replied. "I don't remember seeing one but we probably wouldn't have paid any attention to it. There'd be nothing unusual about someone having a library card."

"I suppose not," said Penny. "And if he does have one, it could be in his wallet."

"Library? What are you getting at?" Gareth asked.

"When Bethan said a younger boy just now, I remembered where I'd seen Lane before. It was at the library. He came in with a younger boy and they played chess. And it's probably nothing, but Jean Bryson told me that a copy of the book on Gwrych Castle written by Mark Baker seems to be missing from the Llanelen Library. For some reason, just now, when Bethan said how much he loves the place, I wondered if Lane might have taken it, but even if he did, I don't know why it would matter." She gave a small laugh, accompanied by a sheepish shrug. "And anyway, for all I know the book's been found or returned by now. I hope it has."

"But if he had a library card, wouldn't he just check the book out?" Bethan asked.

"It's a noncirculating book," Penny said. "You can't sign

it out. You have to use it in the library. And that's probably why it's gone missing. Someone wanted to read it at home."

"Why don't we find out if the library copy has been returned?" said Gareth. "Is the library open now?"

"Not sure. We can get the hours off the Web site," Penny said opening her laptop and typing. "No, it's closed today, but I'm sure Jean won't mind if we call her at home. Florence will have her number. I'll get it for you." A few minutes later Penny handed Bethan a piece of paper with a telephone number and Bethan made the call.

"No, it didn't turn up," Bethan said. "Jean's reported the book as missing." She turned to Gareth. "What do you think? Is it worth going back and searching his room again for it?"

"I would," Gareth said simply. "And there's something else, Bethan," he added. "Lane told us he had a bus pass. He was quite proud of it, actually, and the independence it gives him. If you call the bus company, they should be able to tell you the times his pass was used and on what routes. Their computer should have a record of when it was scanned as he boarded."

Bethan thanked them and left, and Penny turned to Gareth.

"What do you think is going on with Lane?" she asked. "Is he all right?"

"He may have just wandered off somewhere and he'll turn up safe, which would be the best possible outcome. And that's actually the most common way these situations end, so odds are, yes, he is all right. Or, it could be that events have overwhelmed him and he's run off and is hiding to try to escape from what he feels is unbearable pressure that he can't cope with. He's young for his age and trying to escape might be the only way he knows how to deal with the situation. And in that case, we have to find him before he comes to harm. And thirdly, and this is what we hope hasn't happened, he knows something, or saw something, and somebody knows he knows, and wants to silence him. That is never good. And if that's the case, with the amount of time that's gone by, it may already be too late."

Penny took a deep breath and let out a soft exclamation of dismay. "Oh, I hope that's not what happened."

"If they're going to find him, as I said, the first twenty-four hours are critical, so I hope there's good news soon."

"I wish there was something we could do. Can you think where he might be?"

"I wish I could."

The next hour passed quietly. As a silver carriage clock ticked away the minutes, the only sound was Penny idly turning the pages in a magazine while Gareth nodded off in a chair. As the clock struck the hour he started awake and stood up. "Tea?"

"Good idea."

"I'll put the kettle on." He started toward the kitchen, but at the sound of an approaching vehicle, followed by a car door shutting and a knock on the door, he stopped and looked questioningly at Penny. She answered the door and Bethan entered holding up a tattered copy of *The Rise and Fall of Gwrych Castle*.

"Was it in Lane's room?" Penny asked.

Bethan nodded. "You know the castle better than I do. Would you mind looking through this to see if anything jumps out at you that might help us find him? His world is very small so there's a good chance that somehow this place figures into his disappearance."

"In that case, Bethan, you might want to talk to the author of this book, Mark Baker. I can give you his number."

Penny took the slim red paperback and sat down. The cover showed a profile of the countess superimposed against an image of the castle in its prime. She opened the book. The glossy pages were sprinkled generously with black-and-white photographs. As Penny scanned the text, the soft voices of Bethan and Gareth talking to each other receded. The book opened with a history of the land and the family that owned it, moved to the actual building of the castle, starting in 1819, and then outlined the improvements and additions made throughout the Victorian period. When she came to the early twentieth century, she realized she was in the period when Gareth's grandmother worked there.

She wished she could take longer to assimilate what she was reading.

"Bethan, would it be okay if I kept this book for tonight?" she said. "I'll notify Jean that it's been found."

Bethan exchanged a quick look with Gareth, who gave a small nod. "Fine," she replied. "Has anything jumped out at you?"

"No, but if I could take my time, it might."

She turned to the page that ended the chapter in which the author discussed the final days of the family's time in residence. The heading at the top of the page read THE MARBLE STAIRCASE and beneath was a full-page photograph of it, in black and white like all the rest. But someone had taken a marker and coloured the carpet that ran down the entire length of it blood red. The effect against this grainy black-and-white photograph and all the others in the book was startling. Vivid, dramatic, and attention getting.

But Penny didn't see how the coloured-in carpet could connect to the immediate problem of the missing young man. The staircase had been gone for twenty-five years or so, about the same length of time as she'd lived in Wales.

Penny showed the image to Gareth and Bethan who were as puzzled as she was.

"Something to think about," said Bethan as she stood up. "Right. I must be off. Thanks very much for all your help and we'll talk soon. Be in touch if you think of anything."

"She seems more open now to us helping her," said Penny when Bethan had left.

"Because the stakes just got higher. Now she's got an unexplained death along with a missing person on her plate. And Lane could become a high-profile case. If he isn't found alive and well soon, the national media are bound to pick up the story."

"Do you think the two are related? I mean we know that the missing lad and John Hardwick, whose death is still unexplained, are related—they're father and son—but I wonder if the two events are related. A body is found at the castle and now the son of that person has gone missing. I wonder if there's a connection between the two."

"You know how I feel about assuming and guessing. We'll just have to see what the investigation turns up." He gave her a soft smile. "Right. Having said that, I'm assuming you want to go through that book this evening, so I'll be off."

When he was gone, she poured herself a glass of wine

and with her little grey cat, Harrison, curled up beside her and purring loudly, she returned to the history of Gwrych Castle.

As the sky turned pink, signaling the approach of the end of the day, and the light began to fail, she reached over Harrison and switched on the lamp. Annoyed at being disturbed, Harrison jumped lightly off the sofa and padded to the kitchen where his dinner should have been waiting for him. Penny realized she'd missed her own evening meal, but as she wasn't all that hungry, she fed Harrison and then made a cheese-and-tomato sandwich that she brought back to the sitting room.

She read for another hour and then closed the book. She knew who she must speak to in the morning.

Thirteen

The next morning, Penny walked to work under a clearing sky. It had rained heavily during the night, and the sound of the rain pelting her bedroom window had awakened her. She lay in the dark, listening, and wondering where Lane had spent the last two nights. Wherever he was, she hoped he was safe and sheltered.

She had telephoned Victoria last night to let her know she would be late in to work this morning, as she would be stopping off for a short visit with her friend Jimmy Hill in the Llanelen Nursing Home. She made a point of visiting him at least once a week and others in the town were getting involved, too, to make the residents' lives more enjoyable. Victoria performed a few songs one afternoon a month on her harp, Eirlys was teaching interested residents how to connect with their children and grandchildren using social media, a jewellery designer helped the residents with a special craft each month and a local writer was helping them record interesting stories from their long-ago youth.

Penny pushed open the door to the nursing home. Now used to its sights and smells, she signed in and made her way to the residents' sitting area at the back of the building. Where once it had been gloomy and tired, the lounge had been freshened up with a coat of paint. Dusty old bouquets of silk and plastic flowers had been tossed out and replaced by bright, living flowers donated by the local florist. The atmosphere seemed livelier and more stimulating. Where before white-haired people sat nodding in their chairs, an ignored television playing at one end of the room, the residents now enjoyed bingo and card games. Even the food was better. Once, no visitor would have wanted a cup of indifferent, lukewarm tea in a Styrofoam cup, but now the tea was passable, served in a proper cup, and accompanied by a decent biscuit.

Penny spotted Jimmy in the corner, chatting with a fellow resident. His face lit up when he saw her approach.

"Hello, love!" he said.

"Hiya, Jimmy. All right?"

"Oh, you know. Mustn't grumble. But all the better for seeing you. A nice surprise. Wasn't expecting you for another day or two."

Penny smiled at the man he was talking to and then asked if she might steal her friend away for a few minutes.

"Be my guest," the man replied with a grin. "He'll not get a better offer today."

Penny wheeled Jimmy to a corner of the room and turned

his chair so that he was angled slightly. He could see the room, but anyone looking at them would see him in profile. She sat beside him, crossed her legs, and leaned forward.

"This looks serious," said Jimmy.

"A young man's gone missing. Gareth and I met him a few days ago up at Gwrych Castle."

A look that Penny couldn't make out flashed across Jimmy's lined face.

"I heard about that bad business up there," Jimmy said. "A body was discovered."

Penny nodded. "It was me who found it."

"I might have known."

"Yes, well, that's not why I'm here."

"No? What is it, then? I don't see how I can help with a missing boy I don't know, stuck in here as I am."

"It's not about that, either. It's just that I've become very interested in the castle and I've got to know some of the people working on the restoration. I met Mark Baker— he's the one leading the project—a little while ago and I offered to paint a couple of watercolours they could auction as a fund-raiser. So I've been there several times, sketching and painting, and in fact that's what I was doing there when I found the body."

Jimmy nodded. "I'm listening. Go on."

"Well, the more I learn about its history, and the more time I spend there, I, well, I can't really explain it, but I'm very drawn to it."

"You've fallen under its spell," said Jimmy. "That happens to a lot of people who see it. There's just something about it. It captures your imagination."

"That's right," said Penny. "I can't stop thinking how

101

beautiful it must have been inside with its stained glass windows and rich furnishings." She waved a hand in an expansive gesture. "Spacious and gracious. How wonderful it must have been to live there. What it could have been like today, if things had been different. If it had stayed in the family and been lovingly cared for over the years. The way it should have been, and the way other properties of its age have been."

Jimmy made a noncommittal sort of throat clearing noise, so Penny continued.

"Things started going downhill in about the 1950s, but at least the place was relatively intact. And by that I mean the roof was still on. By the 1980s, the main building was in trouble—the years of neglect were taking their toll, but the end came, really, in the 1990s. You were around at that time. So I wondered if you might be able to shed a little light on what happened up there. You were involved in certain, ah, activities back then and I wondered if you know anything about the goings on up at the castle. It was at this point that the deterioration reached the point of no return."

Jimmy had spent most of his working life as a small-time thief and occasional fence. Now, in his seventies and confined to a wheelchair, his past was far behind him. He'd shared his regrets with Penny and they had no secrets.

"Well, you're right about that," he said. "But destruction would be a better word than deterioration. There was nothing natural about what happened up there and the new age travellers were responsible for it."

"Did you know them?" Penny asked. "Did you have any dealings with them?"

"Yeah, I'm sorry to say I did."

"I thought you might have. Well, let's start with that. Tell me, what exactly were new age travellers?"

"They were sort of like what hippies from the 1960s would have in the 1990s, along with travellers. That's the politically correct term we have to use nowadays. In the old days, we called them Gypsies. People with what you might call an itinerant lifestyle. They travel about wherever their fancy takes them and set up camp, usually on public land, but sometimes on private land, like farmers' fields, where they're no better than trespassers. Not to put too fine a point on it, they're not wanted anywhere. They always leave a terrible mess behind for someone else to clean up. And unfortunately they came to Gwrych. It never should have happened. The place should never have been left vulnerable and unprotected. So the new age travellers just waltzed right in, with their ridiculous chanting and sleeping under pyramids and using crystals to tell the future. Made themselves at home, they did." He gave a sad little shrug of resignation. "And really, who can blame them? There was no security. Not so much as a barbed wire fence. The key left under the welcome mat, as we say. They're opportunists and they saw an opportunity. And what an opportunity it was. Everything was theirs for the taking."

"Ugh." Penny let out a little groan of disapproval. "And take it they did, I gather."

"They did. So when I heard what was going on I drove up there to see for myself. They'd taken over the main house and made themselves at home. There was no furniture by then—it had all been sold off—but some of the windows still had curtains and you could see how nice they must have looked. Heavy fabric in rich, dark colours. The place was nothing but the best materials and finest workmanship. The tile work was exquisite and the ceilings were stunning. The windowsills, the floors. The fireplaces were all Italian marble and of course the travellers set fires in them that got out of control and they're the idiots who almost burned the place down."

"You can still see the black from that fire on the front of the building," said Penny.

"Right. Well, they set about dismantling what the vandals hadn't destroyed so they could sell it. They didn't care about the place. They took everything. And when I say everything, I mean everything."

"Including the marble staircase," said Penny. "Did you have a chance to see that before they took it?"

"Oh, it was breathtaking," said Jimmy. "If there's a stairway to heaven, that would be it. With the red carpet. Magnificent. It just went on and on. Funny, though, it didn't really go anywhere—it just sort of ended in a stained glass window. And there wasn't a lot of space at the bottom so you couldn't make a really grand entrance or anything. It was just, well, there, with a couple of floors branching off it. And some railings. There were wrought-iron railings off it, I remember, and of course the travellers helped themselves to those, too."

"So what happened?"

"Well, they took everything apart and then asked for my help selling it on."

"And did you?"

"No, I couldn't bring myself to do it, which is saying something; I didn't have too much in the way of, shall we say, business ethics back then, but this was definitely a venture I didn't want to get involved in. I just couldn't bring myself to do it. So I put them in touch with a mate whose standards weren't quite as high as mine. And besides, that sort of building materials stuff wasn't really what I dealt in. I dealt mainly in jewellery. Small items that could be passed on quickly and not so easily traced. A good way to get caught is to start dealing in materials you're not familiar with. You don't know the ropes and you don't know the players. You don't know who to trust. Anyway, they had timber and slate, that sort of thing. Marble fireplace surrounds, mantelpieces, door frames, tiles. Reclaimed construction materials, you might call it. It would have been sold on and is probably out there still, today, in all kinds of buildings."

"And what about the staircase?"

"Ah, now you see, that was different."

"How so?"

"Well because it was so well known in the area, I told the travellers they wouldn't be able to find a market for it. At least not around here and not then. The police weren't long in hearing about the stolen marble and as soon as they did, they put it on that antiquities watch list they circulate, so it would have just been too hot. Interpol might even have been aware of it, for all I know. No reputable dealer would have touched it."

"So what do you think happened to it?"

"Some of it—maybe even a lot of it—would have been broken when it was being taken down. Smashed to bits. Terrible waste of a precious material. These fellows weren't expert craftsmen by any means and they wouldn't have had the right tools or the expertise to uninstall it properly. They just got hold of some crowbars and ripped it up as best as they could." He raised his hands in a helpless gesture. "So what they managed to salvage intact was probably stored for a while somewhere, in a barn or shed maybe, and then, when things cooled down, sold on to rogue builders who weren't particular about the provenance of the materials they handled. It could be out of the country and long gone. If it did leave the country, my guess would be it's somewhere in Eastern Europe. They snap up that sort of thing."

Penny did not reply and the two sat in silence until Jimmy asked, "Why are you so interested in the staircase?"

"I'm not sure really, but the more I learn about it, I can't stop thinking about it. How beautiful it must have been. The effect it must have had on everyone who saw it. I'm sure the photographs don't begin to do it justice. And I can't help wondering what happened to it." She brightened. "Any of your old mates still around who might know something?"

"Don't know," said Jimmy. "Maybe. I could put out some feelers."

"And when you say 'they,' as in, 'They took everything.' Do you know who 'they' were? Names?"

Jimmy shook his head. "I don't think I ever knew their names, but I do remember this one fellow. Big, he was, and had a big dog. Friendly animal, it was, a Great Dane, I think, dark brown, and always by his side. This big fella seemed to be in charge. Anyway, you could just feel the greed oozing out of him. He'd have plundered the jewellery off his grandmother's corpse."

Penny took his hand. It felt cool and dry, but steady, and he grasped hers with a reassuringly firm grip.

"I'd better be getting to work. For some reason, they

tend to get annoyed with me when I spend too much time away. But you'll be in touch if you find out anything?"

He nodded. "Come back and see me soon. Maybe I'll have news."

"I'd love to find out what happened to the staircase. Unfortunately it can't be reinstalled but it would just be nice to know where it is."

"Not sure if there's anybody still around who might know something, but I'll try. I'll see what I can find out."

She bent down and kissed him lightly on the cheek. After she had turned round to wave at him, and then disappeared, he touched the place where the kiss had landed and as he allowed his mind to drift back over decades, the years fell away and he found himself back in a situation he had no desire to revisit. But for her, he would. Some days, the past was all he had left.

Fourteen

Enthusiastic birdsong had awakened Lane just as the first slashes of lavender streaking across the night sky signaled the coming dawn. In the heavy darkness, he brushed the back of his hand impatiently across his face, trying to wipe the sleep from his nose and eyes. It had rained in the night, but at least he'd been dry in here. He rolled over on his side on the stone shelf that had served as his bed and pulled his light jacket round him. And then, realizing that every bone in his thin body ached, he hauled himself to a sitting position and rubbed his shoulder. The rain had dampened last year's leaves piled up at the entrance, giving them a dank, earthy smell that was starting to choke him. Suppressing a rising feeling that he was going to be sick, he got to his feet and stumbled into the open. He breathed in great gulps of fresh air and the waves of nausea subsided, replaced by a gnawing hunger. He realized he hadn't eaten properly since lunchtime the day before yesterday, when that man and the nice artist lady had shared their lunch with him. Penny, she was called. He didn't know where she lived, but he thought if he could find out, she might give him some breakfast. But of course, it was much too early for that. It wasn't even properly light yet. Everybody in Llanelen would be asleep.

He thought about his comfortable bed and his mother. She'd be asleep now, but if he went home, she'd get out of bed and put on her tatty green dressing gown and slippers and cook him a proper fry-up with bacon and eggs and fried bread, crispy and golden. And later, maybe she'd even buy him one of those fancy coffee drinks with the frothy milk on top, whatever they were called. His father had brought one with him every morning and Lane had taken a sip of it. It was deliciously sweet.

His mouth watered at the thought of a heaping breakfast plate. But he couldn't go home. Not yet. Not until he'd worked out what to do. Not until he was sure it was safe. The woman might know where he lived and would find him there. But hunger was getting the better of him and he had to find a way to satisfy it. He thought about where he might find some food and then it came to him. He would go where the food is!

He loped off down the lane that led to the main road, flanked by fields hemmed in with stone walls on each side. Curious sheep paused to look at him as he passed, but he took no notice of them as he reached into his inside jacket pocket for a tissue. His strides were long and swift and he soon passed through the castle's main gates and arrived at the road. He had no idea what time it was or when the buses would start running, but he knew where the nearest bus stop was so he would go there and wait. Sooner or later, a bus was bound to come along and he would get on it and go wherever it was headed. He hoped the bus would be the one that went right to Llanelen.

The sky was filling with light quickly now, chasing the grey shadows away, and the temperature had risen a degree or two, its welcome warmth touching his face and shoulders. He no longer felt as chilly as he had when he woke up. He was glad he'd worn his jacket when he left home. He patted the pocket of his jeans, seeking his bus pass in its little black plastic folder. His heart started to race when he did not feel its flat, reassuring presence. He tried his jacket pockets but his hands came out empty. With a rising sense of panic he scrabbled through all his pockets again. His bus pass was gone. It must have fallen out somewhere on his travels. He sat down in the grass by the side of the road to think. He'd used his pass to go to Llanelen two days ago, then he'd walked through the town to the doctor's surgery, but changed his mind when he'd seen the woman. Not knowing what else to do, and afraid to go home in case she followed him, he'd walked back to the town square and caught the bus back to the castle. By the time he'd reached it, everyone had gone home. Alone, he'd sat down to consider what to do next and as dusk descended, tired, he'd fallen asleep in a small, doorless space behind the main building. And the next day he had hidden in the woods above the castle, watching the volunteers from the shelter of the trees, only coming out, driven by hunger, when he was sure everyone had gone home. He'd walked the short distance into the town and asked an elderly woman for a bit of spare change to buy something to eat and she'd given him enough for a sandwich and a drink. And then he'd spent another night in that little space. Oh, what if his bus pass had fallen out in that dark place? He didn't think he could muster the energy to walk back up to the castle and look for it. His eyes filled with tears of frustration and emptiness.

He reached into his inside jacket pocket but felt only the empty wrapper from the tissue packet that nice lady on the bus had given him. If that was where he'd put his bus pass, it must have been flicked out when he'd taken the last tissue. But that was just a few minutes ago, so he could retrace his steps and maybe he would find it.

Before he could get to his feet, a looming figure cast a shadow over him. He wiped at his eyes with his hands and looked up.

"Why are you crying?" demanded a woman's rough voice.

"I lost my bus pass," he said. "I don't know what time the buses start running and I don't know where to go. But I would like to get some breakfast." He squinted up at the figure towering over him, which he realized now was an old woman. Her bright blue eyes, unclouded by the years, fixed him in a steady glare. Unkempt grey hair fell below her shoulders although some effort had been made to tie it back with a piece of tattered raffia. She was dressed in a long garment, some sort of vintage coat perhaps, of a colour he couldn't quite determine but somewhere between a dark green and muddy brown. She held out a hand and resting on the palm was the black plastic case that held his bus pass.

"Dilys found it," she said. "You dropped it on the ground just before the castle gates."

"That was lucky for me you found it," he said, grinning with excited relief as he reached out for it.

"No," she replied, snatching her hand back before he could claim the pass. "The luck is in this: that Dilys found you."

Lane lowered his hand to his side.

"What do you mean?"

"Dilys knows you are troubled. Something is very wrong. You can't escape whatever it is by running away. Do you not know that the traveller takes himself with him?"

"I don't know what that means, but I wasn't running away," protested Lane. "Not really. I needed to think what to do. I didn't want to go home because she would find me there."

"Who would find you?" Dilys asked sharply.

"Her."

"Are you afraid of her?"

Lane nodded.

"Why?"

"I heard them. Arguing, shouting, they were." He covered his ears. "And then they saw me and she looked at me strangely. And then he died. And she probably knows where I live, so I can't go there. She saw me in town. She might be following me."

"But you can't stay away from home forever, can you?" Lane scowled at his shoe. "Look, the best thing you can do is talk to someone. I know people who can help you. And once you've told someone, she can't hurt you. Because someone else knows."

Lane looked at her in amazement. "I didn't think of it that way."

"Well now that you've told me part of the story, tell me this. Who died?"

"My dad. He's called John Hardwick. He died up at the castle and the artist lady found his body. The lady who paints."

"The lady who paints. I might have known. Well, you could do worse than tell her. She'll know what to do. She knows people who can help you. People who can keep you safe."

"I thought of her but I don't know where she lives or where to find her."

"This is your lucky day, again. I know who she is and where to find her." The woman picked up her empty trug basket and handed it to Lane. "Here. You can make yourself useful and carry this while we walk to the bus stop."

"I'm glad we don't have to walk too far," he said, taking the basket. "I haven't eaten since yesterday and then it was only a cheese sandwich and a drink."

Dilys reached into the folds of her coat and pulled out a speckled, brown, hard-boiled egg. Handing it to him, she asked, "How lucky can you be?"

Fifteen

Walking toward the river on her way to the Spa from the nursing home, Penny spotted a familiar figure picking her way along the bank. Dilys, of indeterminate age but believed to be in her seventies, spent her days wandering the lanes, fields, and woods surrounding Llanelen, searching for edible and medicinal plants. She was unpredictable in her ramblings, disappearing for long stretches, then popping up again. And she always travelled alone, so Penny was surprised that this morning, she had a companion, who, she realized as she got closer to them, looked like the missing young man. She raised her sunglasses off her face to get a better look and recognizing Lane, hurried toward them.

"Lane!" she exclaimed reaching out to him. "Oh, thank

goodness you're all right. Everyone's been so worried. Does your mother know you're okay? If she doesn't, we must let her know."

"Not so fast, missy," said Dilys. "I don't have one of those mobile phones, but first things first. The lad's starving."

"Does his mother know he's all right?" Penny repeated. "She's worried sick."

"I'm very hungry," Lane said. "I haven't had anything to eat since yesterday and it was only a sandwich and drink. Nothing, that is, except an egg." And then, as if remembering his manners, he addressed Dilys, "And very good it was, too."

"Right, well, I suppose your mother can wait a few more minutes but we must notify her as soon as we can. The main thing is you're safe. We can soon sort out breakfast," said Penny. "Let's go to the Spa and see what we can find."

"I was hoping for bacon and eggs," Lane said, in his high-pitched voice that was now bordering on a whine. "I really fancy bacon and eggs."

"I don't think we've got any in," said Penny. "Look, maybe it would be better if we went to the caf in the town square. They'll be able to give you what you want and we can notify your mother from there." She eyed his face, smudged with dirt, and the bits of leaves clinging to his hair. "You can have a wash up when we get there. And I want to hear all about where you've been."

She detected a slight movement out of the corner of her eye and realized it was Dilys, slipping away. Penny hesitated for a moment, then touched Lane lightly on the forearm.

"Don't move," she said, and then took a few steps after her. "Dilys," she said when she caught up to her, "I want to talk to you. About Gwrych Castle. In the old days. You've been around a long time. You must have memories of the place."

Dilys sighed. "Do you ever stop asking questions? Will you ever leave Dilys alone to just go about in peace, without pestering her?"

"Sorry, but it's important. I want to know more about the staircase. The marble staircase. Did you ever see it?" She glanced at Lane, and then afraid he was getting restless and would leave, she said to Dilys, "Look, can you come to my cottage later today? Around tea time?"

"You're not going to offer me that awful store-bought tea again, are you?"

"Yes, sorry, I probably am." And then she added, "but I can give you a sandwich, if you like."

"We'll see what the day brings. Maybe I'll come and maybe I won't." And Dilys turned, adjusted the trug basket over her arm, and set off to search the hedgerows for that day's natural bounty.

The door to the café on the town square was propped open, presumably to let the heat out. The pungent smell of hot grease washed over them as they made their way past small wooden tables, crowded together, to one against the far wall. Penny gestured toward the sign that said TOILETS above a door. "While you're washing up, I'll order your breakfast and let the police know where we are so they can inform

117

your mother." Lane opened the door and disappeared up the set of narrow wooden stairs.

He returned a few minutes later and sat opposite Penny. She asked him where he'd spent the last two nights but he ignored her, constantly looking over his shoulder to see if his food was on its way. He was rewarded a few minutes later when a young woman presented him with a heaping plate. He snatched up the piece of fried bread, jabbed it twice into the egg yolk then bit off a large piece. He then took up his knife and fork and attacked the rashers of bacon, generously lubricated in grease. He chewed noisily, washing everything down with an occasional large gulp of water.

"Would you like a coffee, Lane?" Penny asked.

"Yes, I would," he said. "Do they have one of those latte things? The fancy kind with the white foamy stuff on top?"

"We can ask."

A few minutes later, coffee in a tall glass with a handle was placed in front of him. He took a tentative sip, leaving a little trace of foam on his top lip. He gave a little lopsided grin of pleasure. "Oh, really good, that!"

As he set the glass down he glanced at the door and let out a small exclamation. A moment later a woman sat down beside him, glanced at Penny, and then put her arm round Lane. "You had me worried sick," she said in a soft accent that suggested an Irish childhood. "What on earth were you thinking?"

"I couldn't go home, Mum," he said. "She knows where I live."

"What you talking about? Lots of people know where we live."

Lane scowled. "I don't want to talk about it. I want to finish my breakfast. It's really good." He piled a forkful of egg on the corner of a piece of toast and ate it.

His mother turned intense, dark brown eyes to Penny. "And how did you come to find him? Where was he?"

"I spotted him walking along the riverbank," said Penny. "I knew he'd been reported missing, so I let the police know he was okay. He was famished so we came here to wait for you. I'm sure he'll tell you all about his adventure when he's ready." And then realizing she hadn't introduced herself, she added, "I'm Penny Brannigan, by the way. I work at the Spa."

Lane's mother ran a hand over her shoulder-length, dark-brown hair, showing grey roots. And we could definitely do something about that hair, Penny added silently. "I'm Shelagh. Shelagh Hardwick."

Lane mopped up the last of the beans with a piece of toast and then finished his coffee. As he set the glass down, his mother picked up her bag and stood up. "Right," she said. "Let's be having you. Time to get you home for a bath." With a curt nod and a word of thanks, the two were gone.

The server set the bill on the table. Penny glanced at it, opened her handbag, and withdrew a £10 note from her purse. There's gratitude for you, she thought as she walked to the cash register to pay.

A few minutes later she pushed open the door to the Spa. Rhian looked up and gave her a brief acknowledging smile before returning to her work. As Penny walked down the hall, Victoria emerged from her office and fell into step with her.

"Is everything all right, Penny?" Victoria asked. "I knew

you were stopping off to see Jimmy but I didn't think you'd be this late."

"Look, I'm sorry about this morning. I spotted the young man who'd gone missing from Gwrych Castle just as I was about to come to work. He hadn't eaten, so I took him to the caf and gave him some breakfast and made sure his mother was notified that he was safe."

"I'm glad everything's all right, but I'm afraid that Eirlys is a bit unhappy. She's only one person and she can't do your appointments as well as her own."

"I'm sorry, Victoria, but what was I supposed to do? Ignore him?"

"No, of course not, but well, you could have rung to let us know that you'd be even later. Anyway, you're here now. And at least you're not spending all your time caught up in another murder investigation." She peered at her friend. "Are you? Oh, tell me you're not."

"If you're referring to the body I found up at Gwrych Castle, there's no murder to investigate. Apparently the postmortem didn't uncover a cause of death, and as far as I know, the police aren't treating it as suspicious. I'm not so sure, though. Something just doesn't feel right."

"Well, never mind that now. Heather Hughes is coming in for her manicure and she really wanted you to do it. She'll be here any minute. And she's one of our best customers, so we want to make sure she's happy."

"Of course we do."

"What's that supposed to mean?"

"Nothing. It's just that you and Heather seem pretty chummy these days."

"Well, for some reason, I don't see much of you lately

120

and I need someone to go about with. And I don't mind telling you I love spending time at her gorgeous house."

"Now that's interesting," said Penny. "How old do you think her house is?"

Victoria checked her watch. "You can ask her yourself in a minute or two."

Penny set out the soaking dish for Heather Hughes. One of the keenest and most knowledgeable gardeners in the area, Heather spent a lot of time outdoors, and although Penny urged her to wear gloves and had given her samples of the Spa's own branded hand cream, her tanned hands were lined with deep cracks that held embedded dirt and her palms were covered in calluses.

Penny placed her client's hands in the bowl and sighed.

"Oh, Heather. What are you like? What are we going to do with you?"

"I'm sorry. I know I should be more careful. I start off with gloves, but they just get in the way, so I take them off and my hands end up like this. And they don't just look awful, they actually hurt."

"Have you been using our intensive, fragrance-free hand cream with its almost magical healing properties?"

"No," Heather admitted. "I ran out and forgot to get more."

"I'll make sure you leave with a jar today and I'll be in touch next month to see if you need more. But you have to promise me you'll use it. Regularly."

"I will," said Heather. "It did help. A lot."

"Good," said Penny. "Oh, and speaking of gardening, I

don't know if you've heard, but there's a massive amount of site clearance and garden restoration work going on up at Gwrych Castle. Apparently they've uncovered the layout of what used to be the formal garden and the goal is to re-create it like it was in the 1920s. There was a kitchen garden, too, of course, and terraces. You're a keen gardener so you could easily imagine how beautiful the gardens must have been back in the day. Have you been there recently? I think you'd really enjoy seeing what they've accomplished. And when I say, they, I'm talking about a group of volunteers. Amazing, really, the dedication and hard graft."

"I did hear about the work they're doing up there," said Heather. "When they get to the replanting stage, I'd be more than happy to donate some plants and cuttings. I've got lots of heritage varieties that could fit in very well with the design, depending on what they're after."

"I'm sure they'd appreciate that. I can put you in touch with the person you need to speak to," said Penny. She lifted one of Heather's hands out of the water, peered at it, then replaced it. "I've spent a fair bit of time up there recently working on paintings I'm donating to a silent auction. The Gwrych Trust is holding a fund-raiser evening in a couple of weeks. It's a quiz night at the pub and should be a lot of fun. You might enjoy it."

"I might," said Heather. "You know how much I love your paintings and if I can buy one and support a good cause at the same time, well . . ." She raised a shoulder in a little shrug. "Speaking of Gwrych Castle, I heard John Hardwick died up there."

"That's right," said Penny. "He'd been volunteering for about six weeks."

"Heart was it? Gardening can be more stressful than people realize, especially if shovels and heavy loads of dirt come into it."

"He was working on clearing away undergrowth, I believe," said Penny, "and the police aren't sure how he died. I think if it had been heart problems, the postmortem would have found that." She reached for a towel and dried Heather's hand. "Did you know him?"

"I wouldn't say I knew him personally," Heather said slowly, with the slightest emphasis on "him." "He was a guest speaker at one of our gardening club meetings a year or two ago. Talked about his experiences working on a royal estate. Everyone was interested in what he had to say. The royals, or at least some of them, are really into organic gardening and we can learn a lot from them."

"Then that raises an interesting question," said Penny. "The site clearance and garden restoration work at Gwrych Castle has been going on for what, a year . . . eighteen months, maybe . . . so why would Hardwick just get involved six weeks or so ago? I wonder why he wouldn't have got involved earlier."

"Good question," said Heather. "Especially when you consider that today's organic gardening practices are similar to the old-fashioned gardening of over a hundred years ago. Natural pesticides, composting, drainage, planting companion plants that get along well with their neighbours—that sort of thing. And if the gardens at Gwrych are being taken back to the 1920s, many of the gardeners working on the estate at the time would have been familiar with the old Victorian ways of doing things. So you're right, Hardwick would have been valuable to have on that project." The two women looked at each other and Heather tilted her head. "So are you thinking something doesn't add up?"

"I don't know about that," Penny said. "But it would be nice to know why he didn't volunteer sooner."

In the silence that followed Penny sensed Heather had something else to tell her.

"There's something else," said Heather. "After Hardwick gave his presentation to the gardening club his wife came to a few meetings."

"His wife. Would that be his first wife or his second?"

"Oh. I didn't know he had two. Christina, I think she's called."

"That's his second wife."

"Okay. Anyway, she came to a couple of meetings. I didn't get to know her, but I do know who she is. Right after her husband died, I bumped into her at the supermarket. She had quite a bit of wine in her trolley. Her way of coping, I guess. Anyway, you could tell she'd already had a glass or two and when I told her how sorry I was to hear about her husband she started shouting the odds about how he'd been murdered and that the police weren't doing anything about it. People were looking at her and she was starting to cause a scene. I felt quite uncomfortable, really, and just wanted her to calm down, so I said to her, 'Well, if you feel that way, and if it's the truth you're after, I know someone who might be able to help.' And I gave her your name."

Penny nodded. "She did come to see me and mentioned that someone had suggested I might be able to help. I wondered who it was, so I'm glad to know." After a pause, she continued. "I think most people like the idea of truth, but when it comes right down to it, the truth is often not what they want to hear. It can be painful."

"That may turn out to be the case here," agreed Heather. "Although if she's convinced her husband was murdered it seems reasonable she'd want to know who did it."

"And if he wasn't murdered, it's equally reasonable that she'd want to know that, too, along with how he died. 'Unexplained' is no answer at all. It just leaves everything in limbo."

"Will the police keep investigating?" asked Heather.

"I don't know. As long as the death remains unexplained, I expect they keep the case open and if anything new turns up, they take another look. I'm just not sure how active their investigation would be at this point." She thought for a moment. "Maybe I'll ring Christina this evening and see how she's doing."

"Good idea. I thought it might be a nice gesture to invite her over to the house, but you know how it is. You don't really want to, so you never quite get around to it."

"That reminds me," said Penny. "Your house. When that beautiful renovation was done last year, were any reclaimed or recycled materials used? Architectural salvage, I think it's called."

"What kind of materials?"

"Oh, timber beams, stained glass, paneling, fireplace surrounds, anything salvaged from heritage properties."

"A few bits and pieces were used in the kitchen and upstairs bathroom," said Heather. "It saves money and helps maintain the character of the property. The contractor took care of all that. But most of the materials were new. God knows, the whole thing cost enough. Why do you ask?"

"Oh, I was just wondering if there was a company around here that dealt in reclaimed building materials."

"There's a big one near Chester. And there are other companies that specialize in brick and flooring materials. Old red bricks that nobody wanted a few years ago are a thing now, apparently." She peered at the work Penny was doing on her hands and then asked, "Why? Are you thinking of getting some work done at your cottage?"

"No, not at all. It was all done up a couple of years ago and I'm happy with it just the way it is. But since I've been spending time up at Gwrych I've become interested in reclaimed building materials. Well, certain ones, anyway."

"It's truly a shame what happened to that beautiful place," said Heather.

"The number of times I've heard that lately," sighed Penny. "By the way, who was the contractor on your house?"

"Oh, he's retired now. But he did a good job. The workmanship was superb and even better, nothing leaks. You hear all these horror stories of bad installations that the contractor never puts right."

She glanced again at her fingernails. "Just the clear varnish, please. I don't need any fancy colours." Penny reached for the bottle and unscrewed the cap.

"Oh, sorry," said Heather, as Penny applied the varnish to her nails. "You asked who the contractor was. It was Ifor Jones."

"Ifor Jones! That's the name of the fellow in charge of the restoration work up at Gwrych Castle. I wonder if it's the same man."

"Probably. I heard Ifor was involved in a good cause and this sounds right up his street."

When the manicure was finished, Penny walked down the hall with Heather and after ensuring she purchased a jar of the Spa's hand cream, and with a few minutes until her next appointment, she sped down the hall to her office. She riffled through the papers on her desk looking for the phone number Christina Hardwick had handed her the morning she'd asked for Penny's help. It wasn't there, so she checked the recycling box at the side of her desk and found it underneath a two-day-old newspaper.

She smoothed it out and reached for her desk phone, then hesitated. She sat with her chin in her hand, thinking about what she wanted to say and how best to say it. Finally, she picked up the telephone and dialed the number. On the sixth ring it went to voice mail and deciding not to leave a message, she hung up.

I'll think through what I want to say, she thought, and maybe try to reach her tonight. She entered Christina's number on her mobile.

Sixteen

"Did you know Ifor Jones is a retired building contractor?" Penny asked Gareth as they drove to Gwrych the next morning. Penny had told him she needed one more day to complete her paintings and he'd been happy to lend his weight to the day's gardening effort.

"No. Why would I know that? And does it matter?"

"I don't know. Just seems interesting, that's all. Him being up here at Gwrych Castle."

"I'm not really sure what you're thinking, but there's nothing left there that would be of interest to a building contractor, surely? Everything of value was stripped away years ago."

"Yes, you're right. There's nothing left. Unfortunately."

"There's the land, of course," said Gareth. "But the building is Grade 1 listed, meaning even in its current state of decay it's of exceptional historic or architectural interest. So he may be interested in or curious about the building, like the rest of us. It's certainly captured all our imaginations. I can't wait to see your paintings, by the way. How many are there?"

"There'll be four. The Melon House, the main building, one of the arches with the swags of green foliage, and a general view showing the whole expanse of the castle. That's my favourite. I have to make sure they're framed in time for the big fund-raiser. I told Heather Hughes about it, and she seemed interested in going."

"Will they be auctioned off individually?"

"Yes, but the same person might want to buy all of them as a little collection. In fact, I'm pretty sure Heather's interested in them."

"I know someone else who might be interested," smiled Gareth.

Sunlight filtering through the canopy of trees and lighting the castle greeted them as they passed through the main gates and drove on up the long driveway. When they had parked and joined the work team, Ifor Jones approached Gareth.

"Got a different task for you today," he said. "Indoor work, not gardening. If you don't mind, we'd like to put you to work in the Gardeners' Tower." He pointed to a square tower that had once formed part of the conservatory. The estate featured eighteen towers, some round, some square, set at random to add to the overall sweep of the castle vista. Some of the towers were shells, built only for visual effect, but others, like the Gardeners' Tower, had been erected for a purpose. Penny's favourite, both for its name and its purpose, was the Ice Tower, built to store ice in the days before refrigeration.

Penny took out her phone and snapped a few photographs of the main building from this viewpoint and then a couple of Gareth talking to Ifor. After arranging a lunchtime with Gareth, she picked up her art supplies and set off for the location she had chosen to paint. Because the day promised to be hot, she decided to look for a shady spot with a good vantage point.

As Ifor and Gareth walked to the Gardeners' Tower, he explained a little of its history.

"In the old days, the ground floor was used as the gardeners' mess. And upstairs, was a small room that the countess used as her writing room. Ladies wrote a lot of letters back then. It's this room we're restoring. People have donated period bits and pieces and we've recently been given an old chimney pot, so the goal is to get the fireplace working again. That's what you'll be doing today."

"What will I be doing, exactly?"

"Cleaning the debris out of the fireplace and chimney. It's choked with rubbish that's been stuffed up there. Probably thirty years or more. Of course, this work should have been done before the room was painted and decorated, but we didn't know we were going to be given the part we needed to make the chimney usable again. So you'll just have to be really careful to contain the soot and dirt so it doesn't get on the carpet or walls. Move as many of the furnishings out of the way as you can. Pile up the chairs and table against the far wall."

"Oh, I see. Well, that shouldn't be too bad. At least it

will get me out of the heat. I'll do my best to keep things clean."

"And Lane's been asking when you were coming back, so I'll send him over to help you. His mother thought it would be best under the circumstances to keep everything as normal as possible. Stick to his routine."

Gareth nodded his agreement as they reached the square grey limestone tower. A weathered oak-studded door stood open and they stepped into a little chamber where a small photo exhibit of the castle's restoration work had been set up. "This is where the gardeners' mess used to be," Ifor said as Gareth paused to examine the display. "We'll just head up the stairs to the restored writing room. After you." A narrow set of winding stone stairs took them to a cosy room on the first floor. A patterned carpet covered the wooden floor, and a small table, with a decanter and a couple of sherry glasses, had been set up just inside the door, on the right.

Light flooded in through a window set into the wall on the opposite side of the door. "It looks as if the original window frame is still intact," Gareth said as he took a few steps toward it. The ornate triple-arched, Gothic-style window, with its centre panel taller than the ones on each side, and each panel adorned with a pattern of smaller arches, framed a peaceful view of fields with the sparkling sea beyond, all under a sky of dazzling blue brilliance.

"Yes, it is. Most of the window frames are still in place. They were made at a foundry in Liverpool and shipped here. That must have taken some doing, transporting those great, heavy cast-iron things. They would have been brought in by train and then hauled up here from the station by horse and cart."

"Amazing, when you think of it."

"Of course, the very fact that they're so big and heavy is probably the reason why they're still here. When everything else was being vandalized or stolen, the window frames were just too massive. The window once held stained glass but it was destroyed or stolen long ago. This window has now been fitted with regular glass, as you can see."

Having enjoyed the view, Gareth turned his attention to the rest of the room. A narrow table, with a tapestry hung above it, was placed against one wall and the opposite wall featured a fireplace with a marble hearth and small black surround. The fireplace was flanked by two chairs with red seats and above one chair hung the portrait of a man and above the other chair, a portrait of a woman.

"Those portraits aren't connected to the castle," said Ifor, "but the photograph on the mantelpiece shows the countess herself." Gareth peered at the image of a tall, striking woman with dark hair who regarded the camera with a serious but vaguely curious expression.

"And the furniture was donated, was it?"

"Yes. Not original to the castle, but faithful to the period."

Gareth ran his hand lightly over the rough stone wall. "Was it painted?" he asked. "It doesn't look like paint."

"Limewashed. It's used in these old stone buildings because it's more breathable than paint." He rested a hand on the wall and looked round the room with satisfaction. "Very rewarding, it's been, restoring all this," he said. "If you'd seen the state it was in—well, there are photographs in the little exhibit downstairs so you can compare. And you'll get an idea what we were up against when you start clearing out that chimney. Speaking of which, we'd best get on. They're starting to dig out the formal gardens today, and I've got that to see to. I'll find Lane and send him to you." But just as he said that, Lane himself appeared. He set a take-away cup of coffee on a side table and grinned at Gareth.

"Hello, Mr. Davies."

"Hello, Lane. How are you? All right?"

Ifor glanced disapprovingly at the coffee cup. "Now Lane, what did I tell you about bringing cups into the work area? If that coffee gets spilled, the table could be ruined, not to mention the nice runner and carpet." His voice was sharp and slightly raised, as if he were struggling to maintain his composure.

"Sorry, Mr. Jones." Ifor picked up the cup and looked round for a place to put it, then handed it back to Lane.

"Look, lad, why don't you take it outside and drink it while you and Mr. Davies go to the shipping container and get the tools you'll need for the job," he said in a softer voice. "And you'll also need a ground sheet to spread on the floor. Cleaning a chimney is a mucky business. You'll have to wear safety glasses and dust masks. And make sure you drink your coffee and get rid of the cup before you come back in. Right, well, if there's nothing else, I'll be on my way and leave you to it."

The three left the tower together, Jones heading toward the area where the formal garden excavation work was underway, and Gareth and Lane to the Gwrych green shipping container.

"Is Penny with you today?" Lane asked.

"She is, yes," Gareth replied.

"I like her," said Lane. "She's a nice lady."

"She is," agreed Gareth with a smile. "And I like her, too."

134

"Is she your girlfriend, then?"

"Well, I'd say we're more just good friends. Have you got a girlfriend, Lane?" he teased.

Lane blushed. "No, not yet. Know anybody?" Gareth laughed. "Did she bring lunch?" Lane asked. "Penny, did she bring lunch?"

"She did. Care to join us?"

"I sure would. I was hoping you'd ask."

They climbed into the container and studied the tools hanging in neat rows and other materials stacked up against the far wall. "What sort of tools do you think we need to clear out a chimney?" Gareth asked his companion.

"Something long so we can poke it up and shake stuff out," Lane replied. "But it'll have to be bendy, so it can fit in the opening. And bags to put the stuff in. Mr. Jones, he won't want us leaving a mess."

"Good thinking."

Lane grinned as they chose some rods and brushes and large drop cloths. "Apparently someone donated some chimney pots so it will be okay to light a fire now," he said.

"Well, that'll be nice when autumn comes. We don't really need a fire today, though, do we?"

"Maybe not," Lane replied, "but it gets cold up here at night, I can tell you."

They carried the supplies back to the tower, spread out the drop cloths, put on their masks, gloves, and protective eye wear, and set to work.

"I've never cleaned out a chimney before," said Gareth as he prepared to insert the rod into the flue. "I expect there'll be a lot of debris up there. I wonder what we'll find."

"Maybe a bird's nest?" suggested Lane.

"Oh, I can feel the blockage," said Gareth, moving the rod up and down. "Stand back. It's all going to come tumbling out in a moment." And with a whoosh, a dusty cascade of sticks, twigs, bones, feathers, brittle leaves, and bits of litter landed on the drop cloth. When the dust particles had settled, Gareth and Lane leaned in for a closer look.

"This is interesting," said Gareth, pointing to a skeleton. "A dead crow, maybe. And what's this?" He picked up the bottom half of what appeared to be a red and white cigarette packet with a distinctive gold crest. He pulled it apart. "And look, there's even a half-smoked cigarette inside." He frowned and looked at the chimney and back to the packet. "I wonder how it got up there. You could understand finding a cigarette packet here," he pointed at the firebox, "where someone might have tossed it thinking it would get burned the next time a fire was lit, but how on earth would it get halfway up the chimney?" Lane stared at him blankly and shrugged. "In fact, how would any of this debris get up the chimney? Or is it down the chimney? Would the wind blow it down?" He thought about that and then leaned over to get a closer look at the detritus on the drop cloth. Bits of it were stuck together and curled. "Oh, I see," said Gareth. "Some of it is part of a bird's nest. Or maybe two nests. The birds built their nests on top of the chimney and eventually the nest got blown. Perhaps the birds picked up a bit of the cigarette packet and used it to line the nest. Or add a decorative touch. Although, you'd think they wouldn't use something that might draw attention to it. And I wonder how long it's been there."

"Long time, I'd guess."

"Probably. Anyway, let's get on with the job so we can enjoy our lunch." He set the remains of the cigarette packet on a table and saying very little, they worked until they had filled a large rubbish bag with debris, including soot, to show for their morning's work. While Gareth folded up the drop cloth, Lane carried the bag downstairs, and with the drop cloth bundled under his arm, Gareth soon joined him. He pulled his sunglasses off the top of his head and covered his eyes against the late morning glare.

"Let's get rid of this and then we'll go find Penny," he said, scanning the grounds.

"They started working on the formal gardens," Lane said, pointing. "They're going to be beautiful. I was watching them this morning. Oh! I found something and I need to give it to Mr. Jones. So if we see him, I will. He's probably at the garden."

"What did you find?" Gareth asked.

"This." Lane reached into the pocket of his shorts and pulled out a flat, oblong-shaped metal disc. He handed it to Gareth, who could just make out the words CAROLINE TESTOUT through the rust.

"I wonder what it is," Gareth said, "and who Caroline Testout is. Or was." He handed the piece of metal back to Lane and pulled out his phone. A moment later he made a little noise of satisfied amusement and smiled at Lane.

"Mr. Jones is going to be very happy with you and your discovery, Lane," he said.

"Why's that?"

"Mme. Caroline Testout is one of the earliest hybrid tea roses, bred about 1890. It was a climbing rose. Pink and showy, with rolled petals. So that," he gestured at the disc,

137

"that's probably a very old plant marker and it tells us what kind of rose was in this garden many years ago. That'll be really valuable information for the people who are working so hard to restore the garden to the way it used to be. It's a very ambitious project. It'll involve lots of research, I'm sure, and this is exactly the kind of information they want. It'll be helpful to them. Wouldn't it be wonderful if this variety of rose is still available?"

"It would be! Should I give this to Mr. Jones now, do you think?"

"Why don't we wait until after lunch? Penny's probably got everything ready so we'd best not keep her waiting." He pointed to the upper terrace where Penny had spent the morning painting the main building. She waved to them from behind the stone wall. When they reached her, she handed them moist towelettes to wipe the dirt from their hands, and then, with Gareth and Lane seated on the plaid rug, and Penny perched on the low stone wall, they unwrapped sandwiches and hungrily tucked in.

"I had a call from Dorothy Martin this morning," Penny remarked as she passed round a container of celery and carrots. Dorothy Martin, a retired American schoolteacher, had married an Englishman several years earlier. She and Penny, North American expatriates with a shared and deep love for the United Kingdom, had become friends when Dorothy, on a visit to the area, happened to drop into the old manicure salon on Station Road that Penny had set up before she and Victoria opened the Spa.

"Oh, good. What's she up to?"

"She and Alan are coming to Wales for a short visit. They'll be bringing Alan's Scottish cousin who's mad about golf."

Gareth laughed. "What Scotsman isn't?"

"So they're hoping you'll be available for a round of golf."

"Oh, I'm sure that can be arranged. The chief constable would no doubt love a round with Alan. When do they arrive?"

"Friday."

They ate their meal in companionable silence, and then, as Penny poured glasses of water from a large plastic jug, and Lane tucked into another sandwich, Gareth spoke to Lane.

"Did you know that I'm a retired policeman?" Lane's eyebrows shot up but he continued eating. "You know, a lot of people were very worried about you when you went missing for those two nights. So I just want you to know that if something's troubling you, or you need someone to talk to, you can always talk to Penny or me. About anything." He handed Lane a card. "This is my card from when I used to be a police officer. I crossed out my old number and wrote down my new number on it, so you can always reach me. If you need help, if something doesn't seem right, you call me. Okay?"

Lane nodded, tucked the card in his pocket, and continued eating. When he had finished the sandwich he stared at the square, pale pink cardboard box with Llanelen Bakery written across the top in a dark brown, italic script.

"Is that cake?" Lane asked. "I love cake."

"It is, indeed," said Penny. "I hope you like chocolate cake."

"I love it," said Lane eagerly. "It's my favourite."

Penny opened the box, cut a generous slice and handed it to Lane on a plate. She had recently decided that everything she took on picnics would be reusable, so had invested in a pretty wicker picnic hamper, lined in red-and-white gingham, with a coordinated set of plastic plates, glasses, cutlery, and cloth napkins, all of which she took home and washed.

As Lane made short work of the cake, and then wiped his mouth on the red-and-white cloth napkin, Penny addressed him. "I was wondering if you'd show me where you spent the night," she said. "I thought about you that night it rained so hard, wondering where you were and if you were safe and dry."

"Yeah," he said. "I'll show you. It's not far from here. There's a special little room. Well, I call it a room, except it doesn't have a door. You'll see."

When the picnic dishes were packed away and the left-over food was back in the cooler, they left the hamper with Penny's painting gear and followed Lane along a pathway at the rear of the main building. He led them past what was once the family's private chapel that had been converted out of a carpenter's workshop about 1870. Next to that, rather like an ordinary back door, was the family entrance that led to the private apartments and then, after passing under yet another pointed archway embellished with ivy, they arrived at the stable court. Straight ahead were the three dog kennels where Penny had found John Hardwick's body. Facing in the direction of the sea were two garages, with chauffer's accommodation above, and the blacksmith's workshop and coach house opposite. All these areas were either boarded up or sealed behind heavy, graffiti-covered metal doors. High on the stone wall of the stable yard was a large round circle imprint where the castle clock had once been.

Lane pointed to a narrow, doorless opening beside one of the garages. "There," he said. "That's where I slept." Penny and Gareth peered in. Thick stone walls streaked with greenish grey lichen supported a curved, barrel-vaulted type ceiling. A solid ledge about six feet long, just visible in the gloom, took up the width of the space at the far end.

"I've seen police cells bigger than this," Gareth muttered.

"You slept there? On that?" Penny asked. Lane nodded. "It must have been very uncomfortable. And cold." She stepped into the interior. A small pile of rubble lay banked against the wall. A couple of crushed beer cans and crumpled crisp bags sat on top of broken bricks and bits of twigs and leaves.

Farther in, almost unnoticeable beside the ledge, was what looked like a brown bottle. She picked it up and carried it out to the light so she could read the tattered label. "Lead acetate," she said, tipping the bottle at Gareth. "Wonder what it's doing here."

"Looks like it's been there for a while," he said, taking it from her and examining it. "It's fairly common on abandoned estates like these to find old bottles lying round, containing poisons and other substances that would never be allowed today. They were used in the gardens as insecticides to kill weeds or in storehouses to kill rats . . . that sort of thing."

"I wonder what this was used for," Penny said.

"We can probably find out," said Gareth. "A good first step would be to know what this room was used for." He ran a hand along the edge of the opening. "At one time there would have been a door here. You can see where the hinges were attached." He turned to Lane. "Did anyone ever tell you what this room was used for back in the old days?"

Lane shifted from one foot to the other. "No."

"Well, I don't want you to spend the night here again. It could be dangerous. I hope you remember what I told you about contacting us if you need help."

"Or if I just need someone to talk to or if I see someone in trouble?"

Gareth nodded. "That's right. Any of those things."

"I have to get down to the garden now to show Mr. Jones that bit of metal you said was to mark the rose bush," said Lane, showing his discovery to Penny. After she had admired it, he politely thanked her for giving him lunch.

"You're very welcome."

He raced off and as the light shifted from the intensity of midday to the slightly softer golden glow of early afternoon, Penny and Gareth walked slowly back to the spot where they'd left the picnic hamper and Penny's painting gear.

When they came to a main walkway with a waist-high stone wall they paused, resting their arms on the top of it, to admire the view out toward the sea. Below them, some distance off to their right, the volunteers had resumed their afternoon work in the formal garden.

Designed and planted when the castle was built in the 1830s, the formal garden, with all the ornamental trimmings, would have been a showcase for an abundance of flowers carefully chosen for their colours, fragrances, and visual displays. Statuary, fountains, and perfectly sited seating areas that afforded the best sea views would have been skillfully incorporated into its design and its beauty would have unfolded, season after season, in timeless, reassuring harmony.

From their vantage point on the terrace, looking down on the Lady's Walk that led to the formal garden, Penny and Gareth watched Lane, in his navy-and-white striped shirt and navy baseball cap, head toward the volunteers. When he reached them, he made a beeline for Ifor Jones. The two appeared in conversation until a volunteer working nearby approached them. Ifor and Lane then walked a few feet with him and lowered their heads to look where he was pointing. And then, as if in slow-motion, the other workers stopped what they were doing and turned their attention to the threesome. They set their tools down and drifted toward Ifor Jones and Lane.

"Something's happening," said Penny.

"It looks as if they've uncovered something in the garden. Whatever it is, it's certainly got their attention."

And then, as Lane slowly turned and pointed to them, all eyes turned upward to Penny and Gareth. Ifor made a motioning gesture with his right arm, leaving no doubt that they were being summoned.

"Oh, oh," said Penny. "I think you're wanted and that can only mean one thing. Trouble."

Seventeen

*P*ale, fragile bones lay in a rectangular-shaped hole about a foot deep. The spade and pick that a garden volunteer had been using moments earlier to uncover them, lay nearby.

"As soon as we saw it, I told them they should call you," Lane said to Gareth. He spoke rapidly, his breathing heavy. "I told them you're a policeman and you'd know what to do. If you hadn't come when we waved to you, I would have rung you." He turned shining eyes to the volunteers who had gathered round. "I've got his phone number," he explained, holding up the card Gareth had given him.

"Just to be clear, I'm a retired policeman," said Gareth, emphasizing the word "retired," "but yes, I do know what to do and it's probably what you would have done even if I weren't here. We have to call the police." He turned to

Penny and said in a low voice, "Do you mind doing that?" Turning his attention back to the group of mostly middle-aged men, but with a few women of about the same age, he then raised his hands and showing them his open palms in a firm but at the same time calming gesture, said, "Now if I could just ask everyone to stand back a bit." He pushed his hands slightly toward them for emphasis.

"What for? To give him room to breathe?" joked a man with a Liverpool accent. "Bit late for that, I'd say." A nervous titter of embarrassed laughter rippled through the group as the volunteers, still clutching their long-handled gardening tools, did as they were asked. Their eyes were watchful and wary in tanned and sunburned faces as they looked questioningly at one another.

"Ifor, it would be for the best if you sent everyone home now," Gareth said. "A police forensics team will be taking over and they'll need the site cleared. You'll get no more work done here today." Ifor went to speak to the group, and as the volunteers picked up their belongings and then, carrying their tools, shuffled toward the shipping container to put them away, Gareth returned to Penny's side. "I hope you didn't mind my asking you to make the call," he said. "I didn't intend to push you to one side, that I would be . . . I hope you didn't feel . . ."

"I know," she said. "I understand. In a situation like this, of course you're going to take the lead. Who else?" She smiled up at him and they walked to the edge of the garden to wait.

"I suppose I could go up and get my things," she said after a minute. "My painting gear and the hamper."

"Lane could go with you and help carry them," Gareth

suggested. "That would give him something to do. He likes to be helpful and it's probably a good idea to keep him busy." Penny and Lane set off as Ifor returned, his head lowered.

"While we're waiting for the police to arrive, I wonder if you could tell me something," Gareth said. "I was wondering about that little room, you might call it, in the stable block. Near the old workshops and kennels. It doesn't have a door on it."

"Curved ceiling?" Ifor replied, making a sweeping semicircle with his hand. Gareth nodded. "That room was where they used to store casks of beer. At one time, when the estate operated like a self-contained village, they even made their own beer. Wine, too. The beer would have been for the workers and the wine reserved for the family and their guests. Queen Victoria and her mother spent the night here. They were given a whole wing of the house. That was before she was queen."

"That's most interesting," said Gareth, as Ifor rocked back and forth, shifting his weight from one foot to the other.

"What can the police possibly do after all this time?" Ifor grumbled. "You saw the amount of overgrowth. That thing's obviously been there for decades. Forty or fifty years at least. And more importantly, how long are the police likely to take? First Hardwick, and now this. We've got to keep things moving to be ready for our Open Day."

"I can't say how long it will take but today is just the start of what could be a long process. The bones will have to be sent for forensic examination. First, to determine if they're human, and then to date them and see if the skeletal remains suggest a cause of death. And investigators will try to identify the remains, possibly through dental records or DNA or even using facial reconstruction. Whoever this person was—and I'm assuming it was a person—deserves to be named. And maybe there are family members or relatives who need to be notified."

Jones pulled a handkerchief out of his pocket and wiped his forehead. "Hot," he muttered. And then, glaring at Gareth, demanded, "What the hell's keeping them?"

As if in answer to his question the first of the police cars drove through the castle gates and made its way up the rough driveway.

"Police resources are stretched very thin these days," said Gareth. "But you can bet they responded to this as quickly as they could. They'll be scrambling the main forensics team now, with experts. Skeletal remains are a complicated, time-consuming investigation." He gestured at the area where the remains lay. "Just so you know, much of this could be off limits until the area has been forensically excavated. They'll want to see if they can find any personal effects with the bones that might help date or even identify it."

Jones sighed. "Well, I guess I'll have to find something else to keep the volunteers busy, then. Shame. We were hoping to get this area finished by the end of the month, including all the plantings done. We have a big event coming up in September and wanted it ready for that."

"The police will want as detailed a history of the garden as you can provide," Gareth said.

"Well, they'll have to speak to Mark Baker for that," said Ifor. "He's the history expert, not me. I've picked up some knowledge along the way, listening to him do the tours, but as I say, he's the expert."

The police car stopped and the driver got out. He put on his hat as he surveyed the sprawling array of towers, walls, and buildings laid out before him. As Gareth raised his arm to indicate where they were, a woman police officer got out of the passenger side and seeing Gareth, waved to him. She exchanged a few words with the officer and the two began the climb up to the garden level.

"Show me what you've got," Det. Inspector Bethan Morgan said when she reached Gareth and Ifor Jones.

Bethan folded her arms and peered at the sad little bones. "So you didn't try to uncover the rest of it. Good. We'll do all that. Hopefully, there will be something in there that helps us discover who this person was."

"Well, it'll certainly keep you busy for the next little while, Inspector," Gareth said.

"Maybe," she said with a slight smile. "Or maybe not. Division prefers active statistics for the crime report. Not so keen on cold cases. And this one looks very cold indeed."

Eighteen

ello, Gareth. Good to see you," said Alan Nesbitt, as
the two retired senior police officers shook hands
warmly. His American wife, Dorothy Martin, was right
behind him, standing beside a slim, smiling blonde woman
wearing a pink golf shirt and a flirty wraparound pink-
patterned skirt tied in the front.

"Penny," Dorothy said. "I'd like you to meet Alan's
cousin Fiona Barton from Edinburgh. She's come to stay
with us in Sherebury for a couple of weeks." After intro-
ductions all round, the five made their way into the dining
room of the Red Dragon Hotel, where Gareth had reserved
a table for lunch. Alan asked if anyone would like a glass of
wine. They all looked at one another.

"Not for me thanks," said Penny. "I've got to go back to
work."

The others declined as well, and when a carafe of water and glasses had been brought to the table and lunch orders taken, Dorothy and Fiona exchanged a brief smile and Dorothy said, "Fiona's recently retired from the University of Edinburgh and has all the time in the world now for golf. She's looking forward to trying out your North Wales course, Gareth."

Fiona folded her arms on the table and leaned forward. Her short-sleeved shirt revealed toned, lightly tanned upper arms and she wore a smart watch on a black leather strap. Penny guessed her to be in her mid-fifties, about the same age as herself. She smiled broadly round the table, offering a display of white, well-cared for teeth.

"What did you teach at the university?" Penny asked.

"Oh, I wasn't a professor," she replied in a soft, polished Scottish accent. "I worked on the administration side."

She focused her attention on Gareth. "I've heard a lot about you," she said. "I understand you were in the police, too."

Alan poured a glass of water for everyone and the food arrived soon after. The meal was relaxed, but not leisurely; Penny was due back to work and Alan, Fiona, and Gareth had a two o'clock tee-off time.

The bill settled, they said their good-byes in the hotel's car park before going their separate ways. Alan opened the front passenger door of Gareth's car for Fiona, and then climbed in the back. With a cheery wave, Penny and Dorothy saw them off on their afternoon of golf, then set off to the Spa where Dorothy would leave Penny and continue on to her B&B to spend a quiet afternoon with a nice cup of tea, a biscuit or two, and a good book.

"How did it go?" Penny asked when Gareth rang her that evening.

"Oh, fine. Always good to have a catch up with Alan."

"The days are getting shorter now," Mrs. Lloyd remarked as she settled herself in the client's chair, ready for her manicure. "Summer is definitely drawing to a close." She sighed. "All ready for tonight, are you, Penny?"

"Oh, I think so. You?"

"Yes, indeed. My team and I are raring to go. Although I must say at first I was a little disappointed in Florence. After all I've done for her and she chooses to ask that Jean from the library to be her teammate. And then for you, of all people, and Gareth Davies himself to agree to join her team. I was that astonished, let me tell you."

"Well, we didn't know there was a problem," Penny replied, "so when Florence asked us, we said yes. If we'd known that it was going to cause conflict between the two of you . . ." She let the unfinished words hang in the air between them, so Mrs. Lloyd could fill in the rest of the sentence as she wished.

"Well, I was never one to let anything stand in my way," Mrs. Lloyd continued. "I wasn't long in putting together a very strong team of my own and let me tell you, we'll be giving you a good run for your money. Consider yourself warned."

Penny laughed. "Well, as all the money goes to the Gwrych Trust, let's hope everyone has a good run for their money, and there's plenty of it."

"Yes, indeed. I can think of one or two people with deep

pockets and I hope they'll be generous tonight. Did I hear that one of your paintings is up for auction?"

"Four, actually. And apparently there's some interest in them. A little bidding war would be nice." The manicure continued while they talked of other things, and then Mrs. Lloyd asked, "And any news of that skeleton they found up there?"

"Not that I've heard. Gareth says it could take some time for the remains to be properly examined. Months, maybe."

"Well, all the carrying on up there over the years, I'm not surprised at least one dead body turns up. The place was completely taken over by hippies, and travellers, and Lord knows who else and they made a terrible mess of it, by all accounts. That body probably belongs to someone who overdosed on drugs, I shouldn't wonder."

"Could be. I expect we'll know more about it soon." Penny finished applying the top coat to Mrs. Lloyd's manicure and set up a fan to help her nails dry faster.

"Although I do think it's odd that two bodies should have been found up there so close together," said Mrs. Lloyd. "Well, not close together in terms of where the bodies were, because I wouldn't know about that, but close together timewise, if you follow me. And then there's you on the scene, both times."

"Now that was just a coincidence, Mrs. Lloyd. And apparently there was nothing suspicious about the first death. Perhaps the man was poorly, and just happened to die there. I haven't heard anything else about it. I don't know if the police are still investigating or when the coroner's inquest will be held."

"Well, that may be so," said Mrs. Lloyd, "but you can

bet there'll be something suspicious about the second death. Skeletons don't just turn up in old flower beds. Somebody must have put that body in there. When, that's the question."

"Yes, that's one question," agreed Penny. "And hopefully the forensic examination will be able to answer it. And, of course, who. Who was this person? That's the other question."

"Well, getting back to tonight, I saw the quiz master coming out of the Leek and Lily on my way over here."

"Getting set up for the big event, I expect," said Penny, removing the towel from the tabletop and rolling it up before tossing it in the laundry basket.

"Oh, I don't know about that," laughed Mrs. Lloyd, "although I suppose you could call it that. I suspect he'd been sampling the ale. What is he like? That jacket he wears with the patches on the elbows and the little bow tie. He looks like an old Oxford professor from the 1950s."

"What does he do when he isn't being the quiz master? Does he have a proper job somewhere?"

"If he does, I don't know what it could be. He's a bit of a character, that's for sure. I never know what to make of him."

"I don't go to the quiz nights, but they certainly seem popular," said Penny. "I hope there's a good turnout tonight. People don't mind paying a bit more for a good cause."

"No, they don't. We're a kind-hearted lot, as you well know."

Nineteen

The pub was filling up fast and Florence Semble and Jean Bryson waved Penny and Gareth over to the table they'd staked out. "I'll get the drinks in," said Gareth, raising his voice slightly to be heard over the crowd din. "What are you having, Florence? How about you, Jean?"

"A dry sherry for me, please," said Florence. "And what about you, Jean? Small G&T?"

"And is it a white wine for you, Penny?"

Gareth set off to get the drinks as Penny slid in beside Florence. She smiled a hello at Jean and turned to Florence. "Mrs. Lloyd was in today. In case you're not aware, she's planning on giving us a good run for our money."

Florence laughed. "Well, I'm hoping Gareth will know the answers to any sport questions, with you hopefully we've got North America covered, and Jean here . . . well, Jean's a librarian and she knows everything about everything! What can possibly go wrong!"

Penny laughed. "I'm not sure how much Gareth knows about sport—well, golf, maybe—but I've got a feeling he's going to be very competitive. We'll all give it our best and anyway, it's only a bit of fun."

"Yes, it is just a bit of fun but I'm not sure everyone sees it that way. Evelyn says she's going to take us down. And I think she means it!" Florence smiled and waved cheerily at Mrs. Lloyd, two tables over, who returned the gesture with a freshly manicured hand. Seated with her were the Rev. Thomas Evans, his wife Bronwyn, and Heather Hughes, renowned throughout the area for her gardening expertise.

Florence examined the answer sheet that had been provided to each team. "We have to come up with a name for our team," she said. "Any suggestions?" She looked from Penny to Jean. "Something to do with gardening, maybe, since that's what this fund-raiser is in aid of?"

"What about something to do with thorns?" said Penny. "You know the thorn in the side?"

"Game of Thorns?" suggested Jean. "A little pun on that very popular *Game of Thrones,* although I haven't read the books."

"Oh, I like that," said Penny. "What do you think, Florence? Should we go with that?"

Florence picked up her pen and wrote Game of Thorns on the answer sheet.

"Right," she said, setting down her pen and rubbing her hands together in glee. "We're all set. I wonder what's keeping Gareth with the drinks. I can't wait to get started."

"It's so crowded, it'll take him a while to get served,"

Penny said. The pub, with its whitewashed walls, low-beamed ceiling and well-polished tables was now so full that conversation over the hubbub was becoming difficult.

A man wearing light-brown, wide-wale corduroy trousers, a blue-striped shirt, and a bow tie, threaded his way between the tables to the bar. He brushed his shaggy hair out of his eyes and then set up a laptop, plugged in a microphone, and addressed the crowd.

"Good evening, ladies and gentlemen. My name is Neville Barden, and I'll be your quiz master for this evening's special edition Gwrych challenge. As you know, this is a fund-raiser for a very worthwhile cause, the restoration of the formal garden of Gwrych Castle. So the quiz is going to include a few questions about the castle. The format will be we'll have fifteen questions, then a twenty-minute break, then the next fifteen questions. During the break I hope you'll view the auction items and bid high and bid often. We'll get started in about ten minutes, so there's time for you to view the auction items now and get your first bids in. Enjoy yourselves this evening, and I'll see you back here in about ten minutes." He set the microphone down on the bar and turned his attention to his laptop.

"Have you seen the auction items?" Penny asked Florence.

"I have and your paintings are lovely," she said. "I'm sure they'll attract a lot of interest."

"I hope so. I picked them up from the framer and dropped them off here this afternoon. If you'll excuse me for a moment, I'm just going to wander over and have a look at the auction table." Penny shook her head at Gareth as he held out a glass of wine to her as they passed in the middle of the crowded room. "No, if you don't mind putting it on our table, I'll be back in a few minutes."

The auction items, with their bid sheets, had been laid out on a table against a far wall. She was glad to see several people leaning over the table, some examining the articles and others writing their bids. Mark Baker, who was leading the restoration project, hovered nearby, smiling and thanking people for their support.

"Your paintings are doing well," he said to Penny when she got near enough to speak to him. "Already a few bids and they'll go much higher before the night is out. We're selling each painting individually, but some people are bidding on all of them because they want them as a set." Her four paintings, attractive in their black frames, were laid out on the table, two up and two down. Other items in the auction included signed books related to the castle, old photographs, and gift cards from a local florist, bakery, garden centre, restaurant, and hotel. Mrs. Lloyd was right, she thought. With the strong turnout for the quiz with its entry fee of £25 per person and the generosity of local merchants, the good-hearted townsfolk were certainly supporting this worthy cause.

"I meant to let you know," Penny said to Mark, "the library kindly let me borrow a copy of your book so you don't need to worry about lending me a copy."

Mark laughed and picked up a small brown paper packet and held it out to Penny.

"I finally got myself organized and wanted you to have this as a thank-you for all the time you've put in working on the paintings." As Penny started to protest, he placed it in her hands. "I've got one or two extra copies. Please. Take it."

As she thanked him, Neville Barden returned to the bar and picked up his microphone, casting a meaningful glance round the room.

"I think he's about to start," said Mark. "Better get back to our seats."

As Penny settled into her chair Florence clicked her pen and positioned the answer sheet in front of her.

"Right," she said. "Here we go."

"Everybody ready?" asked Neville Barden. "We'll start off with a nice easy one. Question number one. What was the name of Henry VIII's first wife?" Jean Bryson named her, Florence wrote down the answer and the team waited for the next question.

"Question number two. In what American state is the Grand Canyon?" Three pairs of eyes turned expectantly toward Penny, who supplied the answer.

"Question number three. The first of the Gwrych questions." Neville paused and looked at his audience, then back to his laptop. "Princess Victoria, later queen, stayed overnight at the castle in 1832, with her mother and their entourage. What was the name of Queen Victoria's mother?" This caused considerable buzz and head shaking through-out the room.

"I know she stayed there," exclaimed Gareth, "because Ifor Jones told me. But damned if I know the name of her mother."

"Oh!" said Florence. "Was she a Cambridge?"

"I don't think so," said Jean. "I think that was Queen

Mary's mother." The two went back and forth working their way through various possibilities and finally agreed to disagree.

The quiz continued until question fifteen: "In what year did Manchester United last win the FA cup?" A loud groan went up amid a burst of laughter. Gareth shrugged his shoulders. "Your guess is as good as mine," he said to Florence. "Sorry, I've got no idea."

"Anybody?" said Florence. "No? Well we might as well guess then."

"And that, ladies and gentlemen, wraps up the first half of the quiz," announced the quiz master. "Now I know you'll want to refill your glasses and increase your auction bids, so we'll be having a twenty-minute break, although it might stretch to thirty. And may I remind you there is to be no searching for answers on the Internet. We want everything on the up-and-up. See you back here in half an hour or so." Neville gestured at the barmaid who set a pint down in front of him just before the first of the thirsty quizzers arrived to place orders for their half-time drinks.

"How did we do so far?" Gareth asked Florence.

"All right, I think, except for the Manchester United question. I was afraid there'd be a sports question and also a pop culture question. I have no idea about contemporary rock music. Or should that be rap music? Either way, I'm useless."

"Anybody want another drink?" Gareth asked.

"When the crush dies down a little, I'll have another G&T," said Jean.

"Oh, go on then," said Florence. "Mine's a dry sherry."

She handed him a £20 note. "And whatever you and Penny are having."

Gareth took the money, then stood up. "I think I'll just step outside for a bit of air until the traffic at the bar eases up a bit."

"And I might as well check on the auction bids," said Penny, glancing in the direction of the auction table. But people were lined up three and four deep in front of it, so she stayed where she was. "Maybe later."

"I can certainly understand your wanting to check on how the paintings are doing," said Florence. "You put a lot of effort into them and I'm sure you'll find it all very gratifying at the end when they announce the winning bids. Your paintings are sure to raise a lot of money for the cause."

"It isn't so much about the money anymore," said Penny. "I'm surprised at how emotionally invested I've become in the place. It's really captured my imagination and I want to know everything about it. I imagine what it must have looked like, what it must have been, back when it was thriving and vibrant. When it was loved."

"Well, it's getting some love now," Florence replied. "Just look around you."

Gareth pushed open the pub door and stepped into the cool night air. He didn't realize until a breeze brushed his face how stuffy and close the pub had become. A small group of like-minded people seeking fresh air were chatting on one side of the pub door while a little way farther along the pavement the smokers had gathered. Ifor Jones, in that group, tipped him a brief nod of recognition and approached, holding out a cigarette packet. Gareth shook his head.

"No, thanks, haven't smoked in, oh, must be over thirty years. Just stepped out for a bit of fresh air." Ifor pulled a cigarette out of the packet, lit it, and inhaled deeply.

"Do you think you'll continue to volunteer to work in the castle garden? We could still use your help but understand completely you've probably got better things to do now that your girlfriend's finished her painting."

"I'm not sure," said Gareth. "We haven't really talked about it. She took a few days off work to finish the paintings but she's back now. And I'm involved in planning the security for the autumn agriculture show, and that's taking up my time." He made a light hand gesture in the direction of Ifor's cigarette. "Have you smoked that brand for long?"

Ifor flicked the ash onto the pavement. "Ever since I started smoking." He let out an embarrassed little laugh. "I heard somewhere that John Lennon smoked Dunhills. Wanted to be cool like him, I guess."

"I thought he smoked Gitanes."

"Maybe he did. After all these years, who knows?"

"Tell me, Ifor, how long have you been working up at the castle?"

"Oh, just about six months, I'd say. I wanted lighter work. The contracting business was incredibly stressful and I'm not getting any younger."

"And did you ever spend time up at the castle before you started there six months ago?"

Ifor's eyes narrowed. "I'm not sure what you're getting at."

"Just asking if at another time in your life you spent time up at the castle."

"Why would you ask that?"

"No particular reason. Just wondered."

Ifor dropped his half-smoked cigarette to the pavement and ground it out. With a wary final glance at Gareth he opened the door of the pub and went back in. Gareth rubbed a hand across his chin, folded his arms, and contemplated the hanging baskets of ivy and pink and purple petunias that added friendly, welcoming splashes of colour to the pub's entrance and then he, too, pulled the door open and stepped inside.

Twenty

A few minutes before the second half of the quiz was scheduled to start, Penny made her way once again to the auction table. The bidding sheets were now practically full on some items, including her paintings. Heather Hughes was bidding on each one and raising her competitors' bids by a substantial amount each time. At this point, she was the highest bidder on all four paintings. Her strategy was to stand near the table and when someone entered a bid, she swooped in with her counterbid.

"Yes, Penny," she said. "They're going home with me. And I think everyone knows that. They're just bidding to drive the price up, but I don't care. I don't know why I want them so much, but I do and I'm happy to see the money go to the castle garden restoration." She surveyed the room.

"Everyone seems to be returning to their seats. We'd better get ready for the second part of the quiz."

"How are things going at your table?" Penny asked.

"Oh, we're doing all right," Heather said with a grin. "We're doing better than I thought we would. Mrs. Lloyd is keeping us all on our toes."

"What's the name of your team?" Penny asked.

"On a Wing and a Prayer."

Penny laughed. "Well, with the rector on your side, that's very good."

She returned to the table to find a fresh glass of wine at her place. As she squeezed into her chair the quiz master propped himself up once again at the end of the bar, picked up his microphone, and began the second half of the quiz.

"Welcome back, ladies and gentlemen. A bit of quiet now, please. We'll start the second half with another Gwrych question." He paused for a moment to let the chatter die away and then said, "Of what material was the grand staircase made?"

"Marble," Penny said in a low voice. Florence entered the answer on her sheet. The quiz continued with questions on French history, local landmarks, gastronomy, and the theme song of a 1960s children's television program.

"And now two little ducks, ladies and gentlemen," said the quiz master, using the bingo calling numbering system. "Two little ducks. Number twenty-two. Here comes the question. What colour are Princess of Wales roses?" Gareth frowned. "Sounds girly. Pink?" Jean nodded in agreement, so Florence wrote down pink.

"Heather Hughes will be sure to know the answer to this one," Penny commented.

Finally, they reached question number thirty and the quiz was over.

"Now, ladies and gentlemen, please exchange your answer papers with someone at a neighbouring table and we'll take up the answers."

Florence picked up her answer sheet and looked over at Mrs. Lloyd who waved her team's answer sheet, so Florence walked over and the rivals exchanged papers. Florence sat down and squared the paper in front of her.

"Their team's called On a Wing and a Prayer," she said to Jean. "Ha! Well they're going to need it!"

"All right, ladies and gentlemen," said the quiz master. "Question number one. First wife of Henry VIII was . . . Catherine of Aragon. Correct. Question number two. In what American state is the Grand Canyon? Arizona, yes, that's correct. Question number three. Queen Victoria's mother was the Duchess of Kent. But we would also accept Princess Victoria of Saxe-Coboug-Saalfeld."

A little groan went up from the crowd.

"Did we get that one right?" Penny asked.

"We did," said Florence. "We might have gone for the Duchess of Cambridge if Jean hadn't been so sure that she was Queen Mary's mother."

The quiz master continued taking up the answers, until he came to question fifteen: in what year did Manchester United last win the FA cup? "This is one we didn't know," said Florence, "but I doubt they knew it, either." There was no mistaking who she meant by "they."

"What year was it, ladies and gentlemen?" asked the quiz master.

"Two thousand and four," shouted out Mrs. Lloyd.

"Correct!" announced the quiz master. "Well done!"

"Good grief," said Florence, glancing at the answer sheet in front of her and reluctantly putting a tick beside the answer. "They got that one right. How on earth would Evelyn know that?"

"What did we have?" asked Penny.

"Oh, we guessed 2012 or something like that," Florence grumbled. "Oh, well, we can't expect to get every question right. And they won't, either."

Before the quiz master could move on to the next question the door to the pub opened. Silhouetted in the pale yellow light from a street lamp was the figure of a woman. Conversation stopped and all heads turned toward the door.

"Well, well," she said to the silent room. "I heard about this little event you were having tonight and thought I'd drop in." She scowled and looked around the room, her small, dark eyes sunk in a blotchy face like raisins in a stiff batter. "Having a good time are we? Well, I hope you're enjoying yourselves, you bunch of . . ." She placed her hand on the nearest table to steady herself.

"Oh, God, it's Christina Hardwick and she's drunk," Penny whispered to Gareth. "You'd better do something."

Gareth rose from his seat and approached her. She swatted him away with both hands and shouted, "And what are the police doing to find out who killed my husband? Nothing, that's what. While you sit here enjoying your little quiz all about that bloody castle, his killer is out there somewhere." She peered around the room, her eyes alighting on Mark Baker, who stood beside the auction table. "Or maybe, just maybe, his killer is in this room." Her eyes roved the room again until she found Penny. She pointed at her. "And you. I asked you for help. And what did I get? Nothing."

"Oh, my Lord," muttered Mrs. Lloyd to the rector. "This is getting out of control. Do you think you should say something?"

"Probably better if I don't get involved," Thomas Evans replied. "I'm sure Gareth can handle it."

"Look, Mrs. Hardwick," said Gareth, "I can see you're upset. Why don't you come and sit with us and let people get on with their evening. We can sort this out."

"Sit with you?" Christina snarled. "I don't think so." She glared around the room. "I'm leaving."

"Mrs. Hardwick, I can see you're upset and angry. Would you like me to arrange for someone to see you safely home? I think that would be wise. Where do you live? You're not driving, I hope."

Without responding, she pulled the pub door open and charged through it into the night. A stunned silence hung in the air and then everyone burst out talking at once. Gareth hesitated for just a moment, then followed her into the street. The door closed behind him, then reopened a minute later when he reentered. He took his seat and the quiz master called for the crowd to be quiet, and continued taking up the questions.

"They got twenty-seven," said Florence when all questions had been totalled. "That's very good." She exchanged answer sheets with Mrs. Lloyd and returned to her table. "Huh," she said, moving the answer sheet closer to Penny, who leaned over and took in the circled number at the bottom. "Oh, no!" she said. "Twenty-six. They beat us by one."

"It was that damn Manchester United," said Florence. "That's what did for us."

"Ladies and gentlemen, please bring your answer sheets forward and I'll be back to you in a few minutes with the results. And let me just remind you that the winning team is sharing a gift basket of four bottles of wine, eight delicious Welsh cheeses, and eight packets of Duchy Originals oat biscuits."

"Oh, that's a nice prize," said Gareth. "I wouldn't have minded my share of that."

The quiz master sorted through the answer sheets and a couple of minutes later picked up his microphone.

"Ladies and gentlemen, I have here the results of this evening's quiz. And the winning team is . . ." He paused for effect. "On a Wing and a Prayer." Mrs. Lloyd clapped her hands together and stood up. "I'll just ask the winning team to come up and accept their prize basket."

Mrs. Lloyd threw Florence a broad, triumphant smile as she led her team to the bar. While the room applauded, the winners accepted their prize, thanked the quiz master, and the rector carried their spoils back to their table.

When they had returned to their seats, the quiz master advised everyone the results of the auction would be announced in ten minutes. Heather Hughes hurried over to the auction table to hover over her bid sheets. Exactly ten minutes later, at a nod from the quiz master, Mark Baker gathered up all the silent auction sheets and brought them to the bar. Minutes later, the quiz master read out the winning bids for the gift cards, books, and other items, and then came to Penny's paintings.

"Ladies and gentlemen, the winning bids on all four framed, watercolour paintings by Penny Brannigan were placed by Heather Hughes. If the winners of all the auction items would please join us here at the bar, we'll make arrangements for payment. Mark has asked me to announce that together we raised almost three thousand pounds this evening to benefit the conservation work at the castle. So thank you all and I hope you enjoyed yourselves. Good night, everyone. Safe journey home."

The audience slowly began to thin as people exchanged good nights and drifted toward the door. As the successful bidders, including Heather Hughes, made their way to the bar to pay for the items they'd won, Penny stood up and touched Heather's arm. "I'll meet you at the auction table and help you pack up the paintings. I've got all the wrapping."

Mrs. Lloyd slid into Penny's vacated chair. "Well, Florence, I told you we'd give you a good run for your money," she said, not bothering to disguise the glee in her voice.

"Yes, Evelyn, and we bow to your superior knowledge," Florence responded with a hint of a smile. "But it was a close run thing. Your getting the correct answer to the Manchester United question won it for you. How on earth did you know that? You never watch the matches on telly. You're full of surprises. I didn't realize you were a football fan."

"Oh, I'm not," said Evelyn. "I don't know the first thing about it. But that question was easy. Arthur insisted on going to the game, even though he was poorly. It was played at the Millennium Stadium in Cardiff, so quite a few football supporters from this area went down on the train. It was the last major event my Arthur went to, and I was so glad afterward that he did. He enjoyed himself so much." She laughed little trills of delight. "And now, of course, I'm really glad he did because it's been a long time since I've enjoyed myself so much. We should go to the quiz night every week, Florence. It would do us good to get out of the house and stretch our minds. You never know what kind of useful information you've got stored up here." She tapped the side of her head. "Well, Florence, let's be having you. Time we were off home. If you wouldn't mind just helping me with my winnings . . . perhaps you could put the cheese and biscuits in your carrier bag and I'll carry the wine?"

"Ouch," muttered Gareth as he and Jean exchanged quick grins and Florence got to her feet.

"I expect Jean will be walking along with us, too, as far as her street," said Florence. "Safety in numbers. Am I right, Gareth?"

"Yes, you are, even in small towns like this."

"I find a walk home just the thing to get me ready for a good night's sleep," said Mrs. Lloyd. "To take the edge off all the intellectual stimulation I've had this evening. Well, a walk and a nice cup of cocoa." They said their good-byes and with Mrs. Lloyd and Florence keeping a slightly frosty distance apart, each carrying part of Mrs. Lloyd's bounty, the three left for home.

Penny and Heather brought two paintings wrapped in protective covering to the table, set them down gently beside Heather's prizes, and returned to the auction table to wrap the other two paintings. A few minutes later they returned, with one painting wrapped in protective brown paper, the other not. Just as they reached the table, Bronwyn's cairn terrier Robbie, who accompanied her everywhere, decided to go in a different direction and as Bronwyn spun round to loosen the tension on his lead, the base of the bottle of wine she was carrying smashed into the glass of the painting in Penny's hands. At the unmistakable sound of shattering glass all eyes turned toward them.

"Oh, Penny," gasped Bronwyn. "I'm so sorry. I must have got caught up in Robbie's lead." She bent over and scooped him up. "Mustn't let his paws anywhere near that nasty glass." As she looked around uncertain what to do, Gareth leapt to his feet and began picking up the largest shards.

"I'm sure the pub has had lots of experience clearing up broken glass," he said as the barmaid appeared with a dustpan and brush set.

"I'll take it from here," she said with a resigned smile. "Nothing we haven't seen before and nothing we can't handle."

Penny tipped the painting to catch the best of the light. "I think the artwork is okay," she said to Heather, "but I don't want to touch it in case there are slivers of glass on it. It'll need to be cleaned and reframed. Leave it with me and I'll get it sorted. It won't take long to put this right."

"I'm so sorry, Penny," Bronwyn said again. "Before all this happened I was just on my way over to invite you and Gareth over tomorrow for a drink. And now, it seems we can add cheese and fancy biscuits."

"Sorry," said Gareth. "Can't make it. Golfing tomorrow."

"I could drop in after work," said Penny.

"Yes, do. We've got something to show you and we hope you can tell us a bit about it." She glanced at her husband,

Thomas, who was waiting for her near the door. "I'd better go. See you tomorrow. And I'm so sorry about the painting. If you let me know how much it costs to put right, I insist on paying for the repair."

By the time the damaged painting had been wrapped and bagged, Gareth and Penny were among the last to leave. As they walked along the deserted street to his car, he described the exchange he'd had with Ifor Jones and how defensive he'd become when asked if he had a previous association with Gwrych Castle.

"I think there's something more to him," Gareth said. "I know it's really tenuous, but the Dunhill packet I found up the chimney and the fact that he smokes them makes me want to take a closer look at him. It's not a brand you see every day. I asked him if he'd spent any time up at Gwrych before now but he was evasive. And you know what policemen are like. Nothing gets our antenna twitching like evasion."

"Except you're not a policeman anymore," Penny reminded him.

"No, but apparently I still think like one and I expect I always will."

He left it at that, and went on to tell Penny about the exchange between Florence and Mrs. Lloyd while she and Heather were at the auction table packing up the paintings.

Penny laughed.

"Whatever happened to 'It's all for a good cause. It's only a bit of fun'?"

Twenty-one

Just after six the next evening Penny locked the door of the Spa, swung open the creaky black wrought-iron gate that Gareth had yet to oil, and walked the short distance to the town square. Turning left behind the hotel, she reached the rectory, home of Thomas and Bronwyn Evans. Bronwyn, with her mischief-making cairn terrier Robbie a short distance away in the churchyard, was deadheading roses. She finished snipping the spent flowers off one last bush and after calling Robbie and tucking her secateurs in the pocket of her dark green gardening apron, suggested that she and Penny go inside. Bronwyn hung her apron on the hook behind the door and washed her hands.

"Glass of wine, Penny?"

"Love one, thanks."

Bronwyn poured them each a glass and set out a plate of oat biscuits and pale yellow cheese. "We'll enjoy the prizes from last night," she said.

Penny placed a thin slice of cheese on a biscuit. "Lovely. I had fun. Really enjoyed the quiz night. Did you?"

"Oh, yes. It was great fun. Evelyn Lloyd was thrilled to win, especially if it meant Florence had to lose."

Penny smiled. "I didn't realize those two were so competitive."

"Oh, I've no doubt Florence will find a way to get her own back," said Bronwyn. "Anyway, just let me get what I wanted to show you. It's in the dining room. I'll be right back."

The early evening sun slanted through the rectory kitchen window, casting a glowing light on a bowl of roses on an antique Welsh dresser. Robbie, recognizing Penny as a soft touch, sat in front of her, gave her his best pleading look, and she rewarded him with a small piece of cheese. After a polite tail wag by way of saying thank-you, he strolled off to his plaid basket in front of the cooker, climbed in, and curled up.

Bronwyn returned with a flat wooden box and set it on the table. "The daughter of an elderly parishioner discovered this amongst her late mother's effects," Bronwyn said. "She wasn't sure what to do with it, so we thought we'd ask you."

"It's an artist's painting box. Very nice." Penny ran her hands along the top. "Mahogany? I'm not an expert on wood, but that's what most of them were made from." She flicked open the two little hooks on each side of the handle and slowly raised the lid. "It's very clean. Barely used, I'd say. Most of them are very messy. Paint everywhere." She pulled a wooden palette out of the lid and peered behind it, then replaced it.

She picked up one of the brushes from the bottom of the case and flicked its fine, clean bristles against her index finger. "Hog or boar," she commented, then picked up a tube of paint. "Oil. Not even used." She picked up a few more tubes, read out their colours, and replaced them.

"How old would you say the case is?" Bronwyn asked. "The owner was hoping to know a bit more about it."

"It's Victorian," said Penny. "Some of these paints, including this one," she held up a tube, "were phased out in the twentieth century. It's called 'Flake White' or sometimes you see it referred to as 'Cremnitz White.' I think it's still allowed in the EU, but not in tubes. Has to be sold in child-proof tins. The regulations are complicated. Nowadays, it's called titanium white."

"What's so special about it?"

"It's a lead-based paint. Can be toxic. But this case and contents," she gestured at the set, "is the best quality. Queen Victoria herself used Winsor and Newton paints, although she painted in watercolours and obviously this box is meant for oil painting."

"How much would it be worth, do you think?"

Penny shook her head. "No idea, I'm afraid, but it's in very good condition and I'm sure there's a buyer out there somewhere for it. Not sure how she'll find the buyer, though, if that's what you're wondering." She lowered the lid and slid the fastening hooks back into place. "An online auction site might be her best bet."

"I don't suppose any of the members of your art group would be interested?"

"I can mention it to them." Penny took a sip of wine. "Although they're mainly watercolour artists, like me. One or two use acrylic paint. This oil is very old-fashioned and demanding. It was very popular for portraits and that sort of thing, but not much demand for it now, or so it seems to me. At least not amongst hobby painters.

"But I can tell you who would love to get their hands on this. Can you guess?"

Bronwyn thought for a moment, then shook her head.

"I can't imagine."

"Forgers," Penny said. "If you wanted to forge a painting by a Victorian painter, Turner, let's say, using actual paints from the Victorian period would be a great place to start. Evaluation experts know the formulation and paint colours preferred by famous artists, so a forger using a paint that was not available during the artist's lifetime sends a clear message that the work is a forgery. Millions of pounds can be riding on whether the paint is authentic or not."

"Oh, I don't think I like the sound of that," said Bronwyn. "I'd hate for this paint to fall into the wrong hands."

"I'm sure you would," said Penny, "as would your parishioner. But if she can't find a buyer for it, maybe Alwynne at the museum could find room for it." She considered that for a moment. "That's not a bad idea. Maybe she'd consider putting on an exhibit of the history of artists in the area. At the beginning of the twentieth century, there was a vibrant colony of artists in Betws and many painters are buried there. It would take some research, but she might well be interested. I'll mention it to her when I see her. Otherwise, Winsor and Newton itself might be interested in acquiring the case. Who knows?"

"Well, thanks so much for giving your opinion. I'll pass along your thoughts," Bronwyn said as she held out the plate of cheese and biscuits. Penny shook her head.

"I should be on my way. I need to get to the framer before he closes."

"I'm so sorry about your painting, Penny. I do hope you'll let me pay for it. Although, to be fair, it wasn't really down to me." She tipped her head toward Robbie asleep in his basket. "It was all his doing, so by rights, he should be the one to pay for it."

"I think we should let him off this time with a warning."

"Oh, he's had that, I can assure you."

"I hope your parishioner will have good luck selling the . . ." Her hand rested lightly on the painting box and her eyes widened slightly. She glanced down at the box, then opened it and examined the tube of white paint. She rolled it lightly between her fingers while she gazed at Bronwyn.

"Are you all right?" Bronwyn asked. "What is it?"

"Sorry," Penny said jumping to her feet. "I'm fine but I've just realized something. It could be important. I've got to go." She picked up the bag containing the watercolour Heather Hughes had won at the auction and thrust it at Bronwyn. "Sorry," she repeated. "I don't have time to take care of this right now. Would you mind dropping it off at the framer in the morning and asking him to clean it and replace the glass?"

"No, not at all. I . . ." Bronwyn spoke to Penny's retreating back as she disappeared out the kitchen door, closing it behind her.

A moment later the door opened and Bronwyn's husband, Thomas, entered the room.

"I just passed Penny in the churchyard," he said as he took his hat off. "Shooting out of here like a scalded cat, she was. Did something happen?"

"I think so," Bronwyn said. "But I'm not sure exactly what. I showed her the painting box and she told me it's Victorian, then she talked about forgery and looked at a tube of paint, and got very excited. She jumped up and said she had to go. I have no idea what's up with her." She replaced the tube of white paint in the box and then gestured at the bag Penny had left. "That's the broken painting. She asked me if I'd mind dropping it off at the framer in the morning."

The two turned their attention to Robbie, who grinned back at them, wagging his tail.

"I suppose it's the least we can do," said the reverend. He glanced at the table. "Is that the cheese and oat biscuits we won at the quiz?"

"It is," said his wife. "I expect you'd like a glass of wine with it."

"If it's not too much trouble, my dear."

Once out of the churchyard, Penny reached for her phone and dialed Christina Hardwick. This time, she answered.

"Mrs. Hardwick, Christina, it's Penny Brannigan here. I'd like to come and see you. I need to talk to you." She listened for a moment. "Now, if that's all right. Good. Tell me your address."

The address was on the edge of town, and Penny estimated it would take her about twenty minutes to walk there. She trotted across the bridge and made her way alongside the peaceful river as the evening sun sank lower in the sky.

She glanced at the trees high up on the hills surrounding the town and realized that the bright greens of summer would soon be turning into the vibrant colours of autumn. The slightest hint of coolness in the air reminded her that in just a week or two she'd need a light jacket.

It had been years since Penny had worked with oil paint and on the way to the Hardwick home she cast her mind back, remembering all the art school stories surrounding that white paint. How artists from the fifteenth, sixteenth, and seventeenth centuries went mad or died slow, painful deaths from exposure to the toxicity of lead-based paints. How aristocratic women of fashion in the seventeenth century poisoned themselves with white makeup containing lead, causing the texture of the skin to change and blacken. Had she read somewhere that even Elizabeth I had been affected by it?

By the time she reached the Hardwick home, a handsome, two-storey grey stone house, nicely proportioned, with an inviting candy-apple red door, she had a good idea what she was going to say. She walked up the path and lifted the black wrought-iron door knocker.

A moment later, Christina Hardwick answered it. She was wearing a pair of floral Capri pants with a black T-shirt and her hair was loosely tied back in a ponytail.

"I don't have much time, I'm afraid," said Christina as she closed the door behind them. "I'm meant to be meeting someone."

We'll see about that, thought Penny. If I'm right, you might find you've got all the time in the world to talk to me.

Christina led the way into an untidy sitting room. A thin layer of dust had settled on the furniture, wine glasses with lipstick smears round the rims sat on end tables, and several weekly television guides lay scattered about, one or two open to a half-completed crossword puzzle. The room reeked of stale cigarette smoke.

"Sorry about the mess," Christina muttered, stooping to gather up a plate with a half-eaten sandwich on it and an empty yogurt container. "I haven't felt much like keeping things tidy." She swept a few magazines to the end of the sofa and gestured that Penny should sit down. "Now then, how can I help you?" she asked in a polite, slightly thawed tone.

"You told me the last time we spoke that your husband had been poorly before he died. So let's start by you telling me everything you can about that. I believe you mentioned he'd been to the doctor and he didn't find anything wrong."

"She. The doctor's a woman and she couldn't find anything wrong with him."

"Okay, let's start with that, please."

"It's difficult to describe, but my husband hadn't been himself for the past couple of months. Just generally unwell."

"Unwell how, exactly?"

"Well, he'd been lethargic. Tired, you know? Said he had headaches, and was just generally feeling low in himself. Nothing really specific. Perhaps you know what it's like, trying to get a man to see the doctor. Anyway, he finally agreed to go and the doctor couldn't find anything wrong with him. Said he might not have been getting enough sleep. Or not enough exercise, which is why John kept on doing that work up at the castle. Or maybe he was iron deficient. She ran some tests and gave him some tablets to try to ginger him up, but nothing seemed to help. He just seemed to go downhill."

"So would you say that his illness coincided with the length of time he'd been volunteering at the castle?"

Christina mulled this over, then nodded. "I hadn't made that connection, but yes, I guess it started about that time or soon after."

"Did you mention this to the police? About your husband being ill?"

"Well, I might have told them he hadn't been feeling well. Or maybe I didn't. Can't remember, really. Not sure they even asked. I didn't think it was important because I'd got him to see the doctor and she said there was nothing wrong with him."

"That's not true," countered Penny. "You said yourself there was something wrong with him but the doctor wasn't able to diagnose him. There's a difference."

"Yes," said Christina. "When you put it like that, I guess there is. Although sometimes I wondered if it was all in his head."

"All right. I'll get to the point. I'm no doctor, you understand, but I think there's a possibility that you're right and that your husband was murdered."

Christina sat back in her chair and as the colour faded from her face, she let out a long, soft breath.

"You agree with me, then. You think something's going on, don't you?" She straightened. "That's a lot to take in, what you just said. I need a glass of wine. Would you like one?"

Penny shook her head. "No, not for me. And it might

be better if you didn't have one, either. But I wouldn't say no to a cup of tea. How about you have a cup of tea with me? I need your help. If your husband was murdered, I think I know how. Well, sort of how. But I don't know why and I don't know who. We've got some thinking and talking to do and maybe we can work out what happened."

Christina excused herself and disappeared into the kitchen. Penny stood up and walked round the sitting room, examining the book shelves. Several volumes on lost houses of Great Britain caught her eye, as did books dealing with Nazi art theft.

"My husband's books," Christina said as she set a tray on the cluttered coffee table. "I haven't been able to bring myself to go through his things yet." When the women were seated, she poured two cups of tea, added a splash of milk, and handed one to Penny.

"Where do we start?" Christina asked. "What do you want to know?"

"Because your husband had been seen by a doctor shortly before he died, a postmortem might not even have been necessary. I'm not sure about the legality of all that. However, it may turn out to be a good thing that a postmortem was performed."

"Why do you say that?"

"Because they would have taken a blood sample."

"Blood?"

"As I said, it's possible that you were right and your husband's death wasn't natural. He could have been poisoned."

"Poisoned?"

"What you've described sounds like the symptoms of lead

poisoning. Doctors usually dismiss lead poisoning as something else and that's understandable because there are so many other things its symptoms could be. Lead poisoning is slow acting. Your husband was probably given just a few grains every day, the tiniest smidgen, and then, over several weeks, he gradually become sicker and weaker—just as you described—until he died.

"And high levels of lead wouldn't show up in the postmortem toxicology report unless the police had specifically requested a check to determine lead levels and this isn't something they routinely do. They rarely have reason to. It's not the first thing that comes to mind."

"What made you think of lead?"

"Someone was just showing me some old oil paints and there was a tube of titanium white, and that got me thinking about lead. We also found an old bottle of lead acetate at Gwrych, which was used at one time as a preservative in wine making, and we know wine was made there and then there would still be old lead pipes everywhere. Of course, if you were really determined, and clever, you could probably find fifty ways to kill someone in an old place like that.

"Anyway, let's assume for the moment that he was poisoned. Why . . ." She stopped at the sound of a ringing mobile.

"I'd better take it," said Christina. "It'll be my friend wondering what's happened to me. The one I told you I was meeting. Excuse me." She stood up, pulled her mobile out of her pocket, and took a few steps away from Penny in the direction of the kitchen.

"Can't right now, Ange. Got someone with me and it's important. Yeah, I'll ring you. Bye." She drew out the last word so it sounded like it had two syllables.

"Sorry about that. You were saying." Christina settled back in her chair and leaned forward.

Penny frowned but decided to continue with the question she was about to ask, "Well, as you told me yourself, the postmortem turned up nothing suspicious. There were no signs of violence or trauma on his body. So can you please tell me why you thought there was something unusual or troubling about your husband's death?"

"I thought then, and still do, that someone he was working with up at that castle had it in for him."

"And why is that?"

"Because he mentioned that there was a man working up there that he'd known before. Apparently my husband did something foolish a long time ago that this other man didn't like and when they met up again at the castle my husband began to be nervous about going there."

"Did he say what man?"

Christina shook her head. "No. And to be honest, I wasn't really that surprised someone didn't like him. My husband wasn't quite the paragon of virtue I might have led you to believe he was that first time we talked. I just couldn't bring myself to speak ill of him, after he was gone, so I painted a rather glowing picture of him. He wasn't really like that; I can admit that now. I noticed over time that people did take against him. He seemed to rub people the wrong way. He didn't mean to. He was just a bit abrasive, shall we say."

How abrasive do you have to be to get yourself murdered, Penny wondered.

"In any case," Christina continued, "he'd decided to give up volunteering at the castle and not go back. He just wasn't up to it anymore. He went back on that last day to get something, he said."

"What had he gone back to get, do you know?"

Mrs. Hardwick shook her head.

"No, I don't. He said he wouldn't be long and that when he got home he'd have a little rest and then if he felt up to it, we might go out for dinner."

"There's something else that I wondered about. The restoration has been going on for some time. Why did he only recently decide to get involved?"

"Oh, that's easy. Because his first wife told him his son was up there and John saw this as an opportunity to spend time with Lane. To get to know him better. To be his dad."

She avoided Penny's gaze.

"Is there something you're not telling me?"

She gave Penny a cool look of appraisal and heaved a deep sigh. "To be honest, I thought his first wife killed him. That cow was number one on my list of suspects. She's never forgiven John for leaving her."

"Messy, was it, the end of his marriage?"

"You could say that. Even though their relationship was long over by the time John and I met, she never really got over it, and blamed me. I had nothing to do with it! I think she always thought he'd come back to her but of course he never would."

Penny stood up. "I know you didn't want me to tell what I find out to the police, but I'm going to have to tell them about this so they can order the blood tests. You do understand, don't you?"

Christina nodded miserably. "I should have realized it wouldn't be possible to deal with this myself. I don't know what I was thinking. Just delusional, I guess."

"You don't seem the delusional type, Christina. You seem very determined to me. What was the real reason you didn't want me to go to the police?"

"Because I thought if you found out his first wife killed him, and you told only me as I asked you to do, I could go to her and we could have a little chat about John's will. He left most of his money in a trust for Lane, with her as the administrator, and I thought we might come to an understanding that would benefit me."

"In other words, you wanted a bigger share of your husband's estate and you were willing to let someone get away with murder to get what you wanted."

Christina nodded miserably. "When you put it like that, it sounds very calculating, indeed."

"Calculating? It sounds a lot like blackmail." She looked at her watch. "I must be off. My cat will be getting hungry. But there's one more thing I'd like to know before I go. Who's Ange when she's at home?"

It was dark when Penny arrived home. As she'd retraced her steps from Christina's home back through town she'd left a brief message for Bethan letting her know she suspected John Hardwick had been a victim of lead poisoning and suggesting she request his postmortem blood sample be tested for the presence of lead.

She let herself into her cottage, exchanged a greeting

with Harrison, and opened the back door to let him out. She was exhausted and could feel a headache coming on. She poured herself a glass of cold water, held it against her forehead, then took it through to her sitting room, settled into a comfortable chair, and put her feet up. She leaned back and rested the back of her head against the chair, feeling her energy draining. In a minute, she thought as she closed her eyes, she'd put out Harrison's dinner.

The pressure on her chest, accompanied by a peculiar humming sort of noise, came at her through a fog of disorientation. She raised her hands and felt something soft. As she opened her eyes Harrison began kneading her chest with his front paws. She lowered him onto her lap and from there he jumped onto the floor and tail held high, padded out to the kitchen. She had no choice but to follow.

Harrison fed, she returned to her tidy, comfortable sitting room. She was glad she wasn't seeing Gareth this evening. She wanted time to think, to be on her own, to not have to respond to anyone, to not have to pretend to be hungry, to not have to worry about what someone else was going to have for dinner, to just please herself.

When he rang a few minutes later she thought about what she'd say if he asked to come over. But he didn't. He asked if they could meet for coffee tomorrow because he had something to tell her. He'd heard from Bethan. The forensics results were back on the skeleton discovered in the garden and she was asking for their help.

"Oh, please," said Penny, her tiredness momentarily lifting. "Tell me."

"No, I think we should leave it until tomorrow. It's a bit

complicated and to be honest, I'm absolutely knackered after playing eighteen holes today and I can't think about anything else tonight. Let's go at it when we're fresh."

"You're probably right. And I've got something to tell you, too. It's about John Hardwick."

Twenty-two

"You first." Penny set a mug of coffee on the low table between two comfortable chairs in the small, quiet room of the Llanelen Spa and then sat down opposite Gareth. He opened a notebook. "It's the skeleton of a woman, aged between twenty and thirty and dates back approximately ninety years." As Penny held up her fingers and began counting off decades, Gareth came to her rescue. "Say 1925. Approximately."

"So that would be your grandmother's time. Your grand-mother would have been there then."

Gareth nodded. "Of course with skeletal remains they can't get a completely detailed picture, and they don't have DNA to match these bones to. But still, they can learn a lot. In this case, they found a bony ridge on the wrist so this person used her hands for a living. She might have worked in the kitchen, chopping vegetables for example, or . . ." he paused for effect, "she might have been a seamstress."

Penny's eyes widened as she realized what he was saying. "And if she was, and she was employed at the castle, your grandmother certainly would have known her. They must have worked together. Did your grandmother ever mention someone she knew who went missing?"

"No, she didn't. But she didn't talk much about her younger days. I wish she was still here so we could ask her about this now." He sighed. "Anyway, the thing is, Bethan's asked if we could look into this. The police service has higher priorities than a long-ago crime like this one and are increasingly turning to nonactive personnel to assist with cold cases. So she's hoping we can find out who this person was, how she died, and if possible, how her remains came to be in the rose garden at Gwrych Castle."

"It would be wonderful if we could do that," said Penny.

"We can start by taking a closer look at the things in my grandmother's suitcase," said Gareth. "We went through them pretty quickly last time and didn't really give them the attention they deserve."

Penny frowned. "Actually, when we say 'we' . . . you don't really need me, do you? You could easily do this on your own and it would be the perfect project for you. You've been fairly itching to get involved again in police work."

Gareth's raised an eyebrow. "I suppose I could do it on my own, but it's always easier as a team. One person always misses things that the other person, hopefully, picks up. And it wouldn't be nearly as rewarding without you." He turned his head slightly sideways while maintaining eye contact.

"What are you really saying? That you don't want to do this with me?"

"No, it's not that," said Penny. "But I've got to be careful with my timekeeping. I can't be skiving off. It's not fair to the women I work with. And I am expected to set a good example for the staff, as Victoria likes to remind me."

Gareth stood up. "She's right. I mustn't keep you."

"No, wait. Sit down. I want to tell you about John Hardwick. I think he died from lead poisoning and I suggested to Bethan that she get his blood tested for that. But I haven't worked out yet who did it, or how."

"Lead poisoning? How did you come to think that?"

Penny gave him a brief explanation of her visit last evening to Bronwyn, the Victorian painting case with the lead paint, and her subsequent conversation with Christina Hardwick.

"You could very well be right. The toxicology results could be very interesting."

"I should get back to work now, but maybe we could talk things over after I finish work," Penny said.

Gareth hesitated. "I don't think that'll work for me. I've got a few things to do this afternoon and I'm not sure how long they'll take."

"Oh, that's too bad. I'm planning to pop in to see Jimmy after work. He was going to talk to an old mate of his, if he can find him, about the old Gwrych days, back when the place was being looted. I just want to see how Jimmy's getting on and if he had any luck finding the man."

"Jimmy has connections to the old days? Of course he does. Why didn't I think of that? See, that's why you're so good at this sort of thing. Would you mind if I came, too?"

"Of course I don't mind. But are you sure you can make it? You just said . . ."

"I'll find a way to make it work. Should I meet you here at, say, sixish?"

"Yes, I'll let Jimmy know. As long as we're not interrupting his dinner. I don't know what time they eat at the nursing home."

"I expect they eat early. So here's a suggestion. Why don't we pick him up after he's had dinner and take him for a drink? There's that new café by the river with the outdoor tables. He'd enjoy that."

Penny smiled at him. "Yes, he would. So would I. And if you and I fancy a bit of supper while we're there, I doubt he'd mind if we ate."

"No, of course he wouldn't. Right, well, I'll pick you up and then we'll get Jimmy."

"And speaking of Jimmy, I'm kicking myself we didn't invite him to join us for the quiz night. He would have really enjoyed that."

"Maybe he can go another night."

"No, I'm fine," said Jimmy, when he was seated at the table. "It's a lovely evening and I've got me jacket. Don't worry about me."

Gareth ordered drinks and sandwiches and when they arrived, Jimmy took a long draught of beer and grinned at them. "Exactly what I needed," he said. "I can't tell you how wonderful it is to be out, enjoying the evening air."

"So were you able to contact your old mate about what went on up at Gwrych back in the '90s?" Penny asked.

"I've been working the phones, as they say. It took a bit longer than I'd hoped to track him down, but yes, I found him. He's not doing too well. Lives near Liverpool with his daughter. He made a little joke. Asked if we were getting the band back together."

Penny and Gareth smiled and waited as Jimmy took a sip of beer.

"Well, at first, my mate wasn't too keen on talking because of you," he indicated Gareth, "but I told him you just want the information. That you're retired and wouldn't be interested in charges and all that after all these years, for anything that might have happened back then. Am I right?"

"It's not for me to make that decision. The police would have to discuss criminal charges with the Crown prosecutors but I'd say he's probably safe. The aim is to bring charges within a reasonable period of time."

"Right, then. Here's what he had to say." He looked at Gareth and waited. "You do surprise me. I thought you copper types liked to write everything down." Penny and Gareth exchanged a quick glance and Penny pulled an envelope and pen out of her handbag. "I already told Penny about the thieving and how they stole everything they possibly could out of the place, even the clock from the stable yard. New age travellers, they called themselves, and I'm sorry this might not be politically correct, but you can dress that up in any kind of language you like, but thieves is what they were. They set up camp, took everything they could, and when the bones had been picked clean, like the vultures they were, they left. Moved on." He took a sip of beer.

"Now the fellow in charge of the operation was called Delaney. He ran it like a family business and everyone did what he told them to. He's the one my mate dealt with. He had a daughter, this Delaney fellow. The girl looked like a hippie with long hair, parted in the middle. She wore those long, swishy skirts in bright colours and had a baby slung on her hip.

"So, anyway, they stripped everything, my mate took all the building materials off them, paid them, and he sold the stuff on. He doesn't know what became of it after that."

"Who did he sell them to, do you know?"

Jimmy shook his head. "I didn't want to know at the time. What they were doing was criminal, not that I minded that so much, seeing as how I was involved in lots of, erm, what you might call dodgy deals myself, but criminal in the sense that I hated the desecration of those beautiful buildings. It was a great shame. Just plain wrong. Looking back, I wish I'd tried to do something to stop it." He glanced at Gareth. "Even if it meant calling in you lot."

"We should have paid more attention to it," Gareth admitted. "Insisted that the owners provide proper security. If it's any comfort, I really don't think there's much you could have done." He brightened. "But maybe there are things you can do now to help." He turned to Penny. "You took a lot of pictures up at Gwrych. Have you got a picture of Ifor Jones?"

Penny pulled out her phone and scrolled through her photos. "Got lots showing the castle buildings and all the arches and stone walls from every possible angle." Her finger continued to swipe across the screen. "Oh, here's one. Not terribly clear, but . . ." She handed the phone to Jimmy.

"Now try to picture him twenty-five years or so ago." Gareth waited. "With more hair and not so grey. Anything?"

"I'm not sure." Jimmy lifted up his glasses and peered at the screen.

"That's fine. Take your time."

"Maybe if the picture was a little sharper."

"Understandable."

"And I think I'd be able to see it better if it was a proper paper picture and not on that little phone. Like this one, maybe."

Like pulling the ace from a winning hand, Jimmy withdrew an envelope from the inside pocket of his jacket. "This might interest you," he said. "My mate had just got a new camera he wanted to try out so he took some photos at the castle back when the travellers were there. He sent me these in the post. Here, have a look."

Penny reached for the envelope and pulled out two faded colour prints. She handed one to Gareth and examined the other. Posing against a stone wall with the main building of the castle in the background was a group of what looked like hippies just as Jimmy had described them: a woman in a long skirt balancing a child on her hip, a burly, older man on one side of her, and two younger men, with beards and long hair, on the other. One of the younger men held something she couldn't quite make out in one hand and a cigarette in the other. Seated in front of all them, her tongue a bright splash of pink, was a brindle Great Dane.

"Wow," breathed Penny. "Here they are."

"He even remembered the dog's name, my mate did," Jimmy said. "That's Ethel."

"Did he remember the names of anyone in the photo?" Penny asked, turning it over to see if anything, a name or date perhaps, was written on the back.

"Just Delaney. That's the older fellow."

"So now we have three mysteries at Gwrych Castle," said Gareth as he lifted his grandmother's suitcase out of the cupboard near Penny's front door. "First, there's the skeleton. Just discovered, but we know it's been there for a very long time. Then, there's the plundering and looting of the castle. But we know they aren't related. The body is more than fifty years older than the thefts so she was buried long before the travellers arrived. And third, threre's the very recent death of John Hardwick."

"Let's unpack the suitcase," said Penny, switching on the lamps, "so we can get a really good look at everything. I suppose what we'd really like to see is a journal or a diary or something like that?"

"Wouldn't that be nice, but just a little too easy," said Gareth. "But let's go through everything and see if anything strikes us in light of what we know now. It's amazing just to think we've got the things we do in that suitcase."

Once again they carefully removed his grandmother's possessions from the suitcase and this time they laid them on the table: the needlework in its tissue wrapping, a pair of round, gold-framed glasses in a worn brown leather case, the dark clothing, the blue-and-silver biscuit tin that contained the photographs, and a well-worn Bible with a black, faux leather cover.

"I remember that," said Gareth, resting his hand on the

Bible. "She read it every evening in the chair beside her bed. She'd be there with it when I went in to say good night. Sometimes she read me a favourite verse."

He picked up the tin of photographs and positioned his hands to open it. Then, with a small sigh, he set it down again.

"You have to be emotionally prepared for a trip down memory lane," he said. "You think you are, and then old memories ambush you. It never occurred to me that I wouldn't be able to do this," he said, not looking at her. "I was fine last time, but this time . . ." He shrugged. "It's too personal. I must have done this hundreds of times as a police officer, but I can't do it personally. Not this evening, anyway. It just brings back too many . . ." His voice faltered and Penny touched him lightly on the arm. "My mother when she was young . . ." He turned to Penny with an apologetic smile. "Look, I'm going to leave this with you. You know what to do. And there's you asking if you're needed."

He stood up and she walked with him to the door.

"Are you all right?"

"Oh, yes. I'm fine." He drew a hand across his chin. "There's something I meant to tell you. I'm going away to play golf. Just for a few days. I'll be in touch when I get back."

"Oh, going somewhere nice, I hope?" When he didn't reply, she said, "Well, take care and enjoy yourself."

"I will."

She closed the door gently behind him, then returned to the sitting room. As her eyes wandered over the items on the table, she frowned, thinking about his sudden departure. This was the first time she'd seen him so vulnerable

201

and expressing deep emotion and it had taken her by surprise. And the golfing. He hadn't mentioned he was going away and it was odd he didn't tell her where he was going.

She exhaled slowly and reached for the comfort of her cat. With Harrison purring on her lap, she picked up his grandmother's Bible.

As she fanned the pages, a folded piece of yellowed paper fluttered out. Harrison took a half-hearted swipe at it as it floated past him, batting it onto the carpet. Penny picked it up and unfolded it carefully. The creases were well worn, indicating it had been opened and refolded many times.

> Berllan Cottage,
> Llanddulas.
>
> July 18, 1924
>
> Dear Miss Evans,
>
> I have not heard from our Gladwys for several weeks, which is not like her not to write to her mother. Is she still with you up there at the castle? As she mentions you in her letters I know you to be her friend so thought I would write to you asking for news of her. I do not think she would leave without telling me. Please write to me if you know of her whereabouts. I do not know where else she would go.
>
> Yours faithfully,
> (Mrs.) Enid Roberts

The ink had faded, but the message, written in a crabbed, hesitant hand, was clear.

It can't be that simple, she thought. That the skeletal remains found in the garden could be those of this Gladwys Roberts. It just seemed too much of a coincidence. And yet, she knew, coincidences did happen.

She refolded the letter carefully and tucked it back in the Bible, then unrolled the needlework. She'd admired it briefly the first time, but now she took the time to examine it more closely. Her eye was again drawn first to the central image of the marble staircase with its red carpet, as the person who created the sampler must have intended. She considered it for a moment, and then let her eyes wander over the other images. A full moon floating in a cloudless sky above one of the Gwrych towers, a pink rose climbing a grey stone wall, a set of keys on a round ring, three arches of different sizes that looked like the dog kennels . . . little vignettes that individually evoked an aspect of Gwrych Castle, but taken together, did they tell a bigger story?

Touching the delicate fabric as little as possible, she rolled it back up in its protective tissue. Tomorrow, she would take it to the Llanelen Museum, where her friend and painting companion Alwynne Gwilt could supply proper gloves, if they were needed for handling it, and the two women could examine it together. Maybe this wasn't such a coincidence, she thought. After all, what is a coincidence but a remarkable colliding of events happening in a way that at first seems contrived or unlikely, but in the larger, grander scheme of things, may simply be a preordained moment arriving at the right place at the right time.

Or maybe, she thought, it's all about the right combination of people coming together, by some serendipitous means, at the time that, for some reason, they were all meant to be together, sometimes to do good, sometimes evil. She pulled the envelope Jimmy had given her out of her handbag and withdrew the two photographs from it. She held the first up to the light and studied it, then reached into the drawer of the end table and scrabbled through the bits and pieces until she found what she was looking for. Holding the magnifying glass in front of her and raising the photograph to it, she studied the man with the cigarette in his hand. In the other hand, she could just make out a flash of red. A Dunhill cigarette packet?

Twenty-three

"Let's see what you've got here," said Alwynne as she unrolled the piece of needlework on her worktable. "Oh, and good for you, by the way, for rolling, not folding it. I've seen so many beautiful pieces damaged that way. Folding breaks down the delicate fibres along the crease." She switched on a task light, opened a drawer, and pulled out a magnifying glass, then slid her hands into a pair of blue nitrile gloves. "It would benefit from a fine vacuuming," she said, gesturing at the needlework, "to remove dust and other particles, but all in all, it's in good shape. It's still got good colour with little fading. Especially the red." She pointed to the staircase that graced the centre of the piece. "Gwrych Castle."

Penny nodded. "You've been there and know all about it, I guess."

"Everybody of a certain age who lives around here has been there. At one time, it was the greatest tourist attraction in North Wales. Millions of people visited it over the years. Hard to believe now how badly it was treated and that it was allowed to deteriorate. Never should have happened."

She bent over the cloth, studying it through her magnifying glass. "A few of the threads are frayed, but other than that, it looks pretty good. Tell me about it. Where did you get it?"

Penny explained that it been among items belonging to Gareth's late grandmother. "She worked as a seamstress up at Gwrych, so at first I thought it was random scenes from the castle, but now, with the discovery of the skeleton that was probably buried at the same time as she was there, I wonder if she created this to tell us something."

"Could be," said Alwynne. "If someone with a talent for writing wanted to record something, she'd write it. You or I might paint it. And this lady," she gestured at the cloth, "might use her needle skills to express herself. We have to remember that back then many people left school early and didn't have the advantage of a lot of education, so writing might not have been easy for her. What do you think she was trying to tell us?"

"Rather than my telling you what I think, with that bit of information I just gave you, why don't we try to piece together what this needlework might be trying to tell us? Let's just talk it through and see what we come up with."

"Well, the focal point of the piece is the stunning marble staircase with its red carpet. So we're meant to start there.

Whatever story this piece of needlework holds, it took place at Gwrych Castle."

"I wish I could have seen that staircase," said Penny. "Did you see it?"

"I did. It was in pretty rough shape by then, though. People had chipped away at it, taking away bits as souvenirs, if you can believe." Penny made a little tsk of disgust. "I know. Anyway, this carpeted staircase in the centre establishes Gwrych Castle without a doubt as the place." She pointed to the items in the top left corner. "A moon above a square tower. Night? And you could probably work out which tower this is. Then, we have pink flowers against a wall, is it? A climbing rose, possibly. Summer?" Penny said nothing about the body being discovered in the old formal rose garden and Alwynne moved on. "Keys. Keys to the castle? Who would have had keys? Someone in authority, a position of trust. Butler? Housekeeper?"

"I think the keys on a ring exclude the housekeeper," said Penny. "Her keys would probably have been worn on a little chain hanging from her belt. It's called a chatelaine. I know this because there's a Canadian women's magazine by that name."

"You're right. Okay, so not the housekeeper. Maybe the butler."

"Or, this just occurred to me," said Penny, her voice rising with excitement. "Gardener. That would tie in with the roses and there was a gardeners' tower, so presumably there would have been keys. And come to think of it, the Gardeners' Tower is square."

"Gardeners would have had pesticides they'd want to

keep locked up," Alwynne said. "So presumably the head gardener would have had a set of keys. They used a lot of dangerous chemicals back then that would never be allowed today. And ridiculously easy to get, they were, too."

"That's exactly what Gareth said when we found some," said Penny. "It wasn't a gardening pesticide, but something that might have been used in wine making. Found it in what used to be a little room where beer and ale was stored."

"So we have a person in a position of authority—that's what the keys represent—and then something in the rose garden, possibly at night. Is that it? What about this arch? There's what looks like a stick here." She lifted her magnifying glass and took a closer look. "Oh! I think it's a rake. And if you look closer, there's a spade as well."

"Oh, my goodness," said Penny. "That's what this is all about! It is the story of that skeleton discovered in the rose garden at Gwrych. Like I said, it's been dated to the 1920s, when Gareth's grandmother was there. We found this needlepoint in amongst her personal effects, but discovering this so soon after the skeleton was found seemed like such a coincidence."

"Often things seem like a coincidence," said Alwyn, "but when you're dealing with matters from the past, with historical events and objects, you realize that it's not a coincidence at all. It's meant to be. Look at the discovery of the remains of Richard III—the historian who did the research was standing in the parking space, which just happened to be marked with an R, not the Q spot or the S spot and that's exactly where King Richard's remains were found.

"And then there was the descendent on his mother's side who just happened to be the last of the line and who was the only person who could provide the DNA to confirm the remains were really Richard III—and incidentally the descendent just happened to be a carpenter, so he could make the coffin . . . any one of these things would seem like an impossible coincidence and yet they all happened." She opened her hands in an expansive gesture. "And not only did they happen, but they all happened at the right time and in the right order, so everything could come together. Twenty-five years or so either way and it couldn't have happened. Twenty-five years ago they didn't have the DNA capability to prove the bones belonged to Richard III and twenty-five years from now, there would have been no one alive to provide that DNA."

She shook her head firmly. "No, I do not believe the discovery of this needlework is a coincidence. I believe it happened when it was meant to. It was the right time." She turned back to the needlepoint. "Let's see what else we have. We don't want to miss anything." She pored over the fabric again, then straightened up. "Do the initials GR mean anything to you?"

Penny started. *Gladwys Roberts.* "Yes, they do. Why? What do you see?"

"Well, just look how she's worked the name Gwrych. The G is a capital letter as you'd expect, but the capital R?"

"I think she was telling us that Gladwys Roberts was murdered and placed in a shallow grave in the rose garden. I think we know that now. The questions are how? And who? That's what we need to find out." Penny looked at her watch and gasped. "Oh, no. I'm late for work. Victoria's going to be hopping!" Alwynne hastily rolled up the needlework and handed it to Penny.

"Let me know how you get on," she said. "I'll be in touch if anything else comes to mind."

"Yes, please do and thanks," Penny said as she hurried out the door. She raced down the cobblestone street behind the hotel, rounded the corner into the town square, and then pushed open the gate to the Spa. Just ten minutes late. Not too bad.

She pushed open the door to be greeted by a smiling Rhian. "Morning, Penny."

Penny returned home from work that evening to find Dilys the wanderer waiting for her in the small meadow across the lane from her cottage. Penny strolled over to her.

"Hello, Dilys. You look quite a picture standing there. In fact, I'd like to take a photo or two right now while the light is still good so I can paint this later. Would that be all right?"

"I guess so."

Dilys stared straight ahead while Penny took a couple of photographs of her standing stiffly in among the wildflowers in purples, white, and yellows and waving grasses up to her knees. She then shifted her overflowing trug basket to the other arm and they walked to Penny's cottage.

"I've come for that cup of tea," she said. "I couldn't come before, when you wanted to talk to me about Gwrych Castle. I've been busy. But now I want to tell you something. I know something."

"Do you, Dilys?" Penny said as she unlocked the door. "I thought about you and hoped you'd come to see me, but

I knew you'd be here when the time was right for you. Just set your basket down there and we'll go through to the kitchen."

"You'd better put the kettle on. We'll need some of that awful tea you promised me." While the tea was steeping, they sat at the kitchen table, and Dilys heaved a heavy sigh.

"It's about that skeleton that was found up at Gwrych," Dilys began. "Many years ago, my brother Pawl, God rest his soul, told me something had happened up there. You remember Pawl. He was the head gardener at Ty Brith Hall for many years."

Penny nodded. "Yes, I do remember him." Ty Brith Hall was a beautiful country house situated on a hill overlooking the town and while not nearly as grand or picturesque as Gwrych Castle had once been, it was nevertheless a charming and well-maintained property.

"Well, he had a lot of respect for the Gwrych gardeners, Pawl did. They really knew what they were about, my brother used to say. They started young and got the best training. They were very knowledgeable about every aspect of what it takes to maintain a country house garden. Vegetables, trees, and flowers. Especially roses. The Gwrych roses were second to none." Penny reached for the teapot and poured two cups. "So over the years, as the Gwrych estate wound down and the workers were let go, whenever Gwrych gardeners came to him looking for work, my brother always hired them, if he could. Sometimes it was just seasonal, sometimes he took them on permanent like." She took a sip of her tea. "So he gave one fellow from Gwrych a job, an older man he was, almost retirement age, and they

211

got to be friends. And one night, when they'd both had a bit to drink, the fellow told him a story of something that had happened up there when he'd just started working at Gwrych. He was just a scrap of a boy, you understand. Thirteen or maybe fourteen at the time, he was. He said one of the staff, a young woman, went missing. And then . . ."

Penny's heart began to beat a little faster.

Twenty-four

July 1924
Gwrych Castle

*I*t was the noise coming from the garden that woke the boy. When you work in a garden, you hear that sound all day long, so he knew what it was. A heavy boot being positioned on top of a spade, the soft grunt as the implement is driven into the earth by the full weight of a man and the soft, yet heavy thud of dirt landing on dirt. And again and again.

Someone was digging.

He propped himself up on his elbows and stared at the inky night sky visible through the small window high above him. Slowly, he eased himself up off the thin mattress on the floor of the Gardeners' Tower and gently pushed on the wooden door. It swung open on its wrought-iron hinges, letting in the heady fragrance of night-blooming flowers. The air felt cool on his bare legs beneath his blue-and-white night shirt. It must be past midnight, he thought, maybe two in the morning. Who could be digging at this hour?

In the pale moonlight he could just make out two shadowy figures at the far end of the rose garden. He stepped out of the tower and trailing his hand along the terrace wall, he crept toward them. The light from a lantern on the ground cast the men's shapes into shadowy relief. One stood to one side, leaning on his shovel as the other struggled to lift something big and bulky out of a wheelbarrow. The other man lay down his spade and grasping the bundle at the other end, together they managed to lift it clear of the wheelbarrow. Swinging it gently, they heaved it into the hole the man had dug. They paused for a moment, as if to catch their breath, and exchanged a few words in low tones. The boy wasn't close enough to hear what they were saying. After a few minutes they seemed to recover from their exertions and each taking a spade, they shoveled the dirt back where it had come from.

The boy slunk back along the wall and returned to his bed, but not to sleep. He lay on his back, staring into the darkness until the sky began to lighten and the room turned from black to grey.

The next morning, he placed a few plants in the wheelbarrow, and on the pretext of delivering the plants to his supervisor, trundled along the terrace to the rose garden. He hoped he wouldn't meet a senior staff member on the way who would demand to know what business he had using the formal walkway where a member of the family might happen along at any moment.

When he reached the spot where the two men had been digging, he released his grip on the wooden handles and set the wheelbarrow down on the grass. He peered into the flower bed and at first, he saw nothing out of the ordinary, but when he looked closer, he realized that several rose bushes were not as large as their neighbours and the soil mounded round their roots was loosely packed.

Pushing the wheelbarrow, he returned to the stable yard where the outdoor workers were finishing their midmorning tea break. Just as the clock on the brick wall above the carriage house reached the hour, a kitchen maid appeared with a tray and gathered up their used mugs. Shouting and joking to one another, the grooms returned to the stable and the blacksmith disappeared into his forge. The gardeners, the last to leave, were just setting off when a young woman in a tidy black dress and black oxford shoes emerged from the staff entrance of the main house. Her auburn hair framed her face in soft waves. The boy could tell from the quality of her dress that she wasn't a housemaid, but she wasn't a member of the family, either. She made her way across the cobblestones, treading carefully on the rough surface. She gave him a quick smile revealing even, white teeth, and he watched as she opened the door to the laundry and vanished into a cloud of steam.

"Who is that?" he asked the man beside him.

"That's Annie Evans. She's one of the seamstresses," he replied. "And never you mind gawping at her. She's much too fine for the likes of you. Now get off to the vegetable garden. When you've finished weeding the onions you can cut some lettuce and bring it round to the kitchen door. Cook'll be wanting it for the lunchtime sandwiches."

The silence in Penny's kitchen when Dilys finished describing the events as told to her by her brother was broken only by the soft ticking of a clock in another room.

"The young woman who disappeared, do you know what her name was?" asked Penny.

"No, I don't. But the gardener's boy said this other young woman, a seamstress called Annie, I think it was, was a friend of the missing girl and she was trying to find her. Went round asking questions like a proper little detective."

"And this gardener's boy, do you know his name?"

"No, but he's been dead a long time, I would think. It was a long time ago he worked for my brother."

"And I don't suppose he happened to mention the names of the two men he saw digging in the garden that night?"

Dilys shook her head mournfully.

"I wonder if the boy ever reported what he saw to anyone."

"Who would he tell?" said Dilys. "He was just a lad. The men doing the digging were more senior than he was. He was probably working to support his mother and younger brothers and sisters and he couldn't risk losing his job. And you have to remember how young people were treated in those days. Nobody would have listened to him and he'd have probably been given a right good hiding into the bargain." She let out a long, despondent sigh. "Anyway, I don't know any more than that, remembered as best I could, but I

216

thought I'd pass it on. I knew you'd be interested. Do what you think best with the information. And now I think it's time I was . . ."

"Wait," said Penny, jumping up from the table. "You can't go yet. I want to show you something. I think the boy did tell someone. Pour yourself another cup of tea and I'll be right back."

"No, thank you. One cup of your tea is quite enough for me."

Penny returned with the needlework and carefully rolled it out on the table, leaving it sitting on top of its protective tissue paper. To Penny's relief, Dilys folded her hands, which were deeply embedded with dirt from her foraging, and rested them in her lap, leaning forward to study the embroidered piece of work.

"I see," she said. "The staircase, the towers, the garden, the moonlight. Yes, it all fits with the story the fellow told my brother. Who did this, do you know?"

"Annie Evans," Penny said. "She was actually Gareth's grandmother."

"Was she really? That's very interesting. Well now I've given you lots to think about."

"Yes, you certainly have."

"That's all I had to say, really, so I'll be on my way." She eyed the fruit bowl. "But I'll take some fruit with me, if you don't mind." Penny slid the bowl closer and Dilys helped herself to two bananas, then stood up and moved to the back door.

"I might as well go out this way since it's closer," she said, disappearing into the evening through the kitchen door. Penny closed it behind her and turned the key in the lock.

She considered ringing Det. Inspector Bethan Morgan to tell her what she'd learned about the possible identity of the skeleton in the Gwrych rose garden, but on second thought, decided to hold off until she'd told Gareth what Dilys had shared. It was his grandmother, after all, who had probably been involved and who had created the needlework.

As she set about preparing a light supper, she checked her phone. Now that she thought about it, it seemed odd she hadn't heard from him for a few days.

Twenty-five

Got a minute?" she said to Victoria.

"I do. I was just about to go upstairs for lunch. Want to join me? It'll just be a quick ham and tomato sandwich and a cup of tea. I've got an appointment this afternoon with a new supplier."

"Sounds great."

During the Spa's renovation, a charming flat had been created on the top floor for Victoria. She had decorated it in a chic English country house style and with its soft colours, comfortable furniture, handsome prints, and stunning views over the River Conwy, it was cosy and sophisticated at the same time.

Victoria plugged in the kettle and while the water heated, made sandwiches, cut them into four, and plated them. "Put these on the table and I'll join you in a minute with the tea.

"What's up?" she asked when they were seated. She took a bite of her sandwich and raised an inquisitive eyebrow.

"I'm not sure," said Penny, picking up a sandwich. "There's just so much going on in my life right now and it seems ages since you and I had a proper chat. I miss the old days when we talked about everything."

"So do I. And it's not like we had a falling out or anything. We've just been neglecting each other lately."

"Well, you seem to be spending a lot of time with Heather Hughes."

"You said that before and I told you it's just because you seem to be spending more time with Gareth."

"I was afraid you might like Heather more than you like me."

"I could never like anyone more than I like you."

Penny smiled. "Good. Now it's actually Gareth that I want to talk to you about. He told me a few days ago he was going golfing and then I didn't hear from him. But I did get a text from him saying he expected to be back late this afternoon."

"Well, that's all right, then."

"Maybe." Penny set the untouched sandwich on her plate. "The thing is, before he left I asked him where he was going to play golf and he didn't tell me."

Victoria shrugged. "Could be all kinds of reasons. And anyway, aren't you just friends? So does he really have to tell you where he's going?"

"I suppose not, but it just didn't seem like him, that's all."

"Well, he'll probably tell you all about it when you see him this evening," Victoria said. "Now eat your lunch, there's a good girl. I'm meeting this sales rep, remember, and

I don't want to be late. I hope he's going to offer us a good price on products for the hair salon. There's a new line of shampoo our clients might like. It's made with aloevera cactus from Arizona."

Penny unlocked the door to her cottage that evening and set her handbag on the bottom stair. She stepped into the sitting room and gasped when she looked through to the kitchen. The back door was wide open. With her heart beginning to pound, she looked around wildly to see if anything had been taken and while she hesitated, uncertain if she should leave quietly by the front door and ring the police, or creep into the kitchen and investigate, a familiar male voice drifted in through the open back door.

"It's all right," he said. "Don't worry. It's only me."

"What are you doing here?" Penny demanded as Gareth walked through the door and into the kitchen. "I wasn't expecting you. God, you gave me a terrible fright. I thought I'd been burgled." He knew where she hid the spare key and she thought he must have used it to enter the cottage while she was at work.

"You left your back door unlocked when you went to work this morning," he said. He was wearing the old blue jeans and tattered shirt with the small blue and white check pattern that he'd worn at Gwrych Castle. His hands were dirty. "I opened it to let Harrison out. He's been keeping me company."

He tipped his head at the sink and when she nodded, he turned on the tap, squirted a generous amount of liquid soap on his hands and lathered them up. "I hate to see an unlocked door," he said over his shoulder as he rubbed his hands together. "You can see how easy it would be for an intruder to get in."

Penny peered through the kitchen door at a spade leaning against her garden wall beside a pile of freshly mounded dirt with what looked like a sickly branch with a few limp leaves on straggly twigs.

"What's all that?" she asked.

"Got you a present," Gareth responded as he dried his hands.

"What is it?"

"Come and let me show you." They stepped out into the small area at the rear of the cottage bounded by a stone wall that separated the property from the fields beyond. "I've just planted three Mme. Caroline Testout rose bushes for you. The same ones found in the rose garden at Gwrych Castle. There's another one just there," he said pointing along the wall. "And there. One day, when they've had time to grow together, that wall should be covered in climbing pink roses."

"Oh, that'll be lovely," she said, smiling at him. "What a beautiful, thoughtful gift. Thank you. I'll think of you every time I look at them."

"Let's sit down, shall we? If you don't mind me in these clothes. There's something I'd like to tell you."

"I've got things to tell you, too. Dilys has been to see me. Her brother told her a story about the garden, and I found something in your grandmother's Bible. I was going to tell Bethan, but I realized I should wait until you got back. Let me just get the letter." As she turned away, he grasped her lightly on her forearm.

222

"Penny."

Something in his tone brought her up short.

"What is it? Is everything all right?"

"Everything's fine. Let's sit down."

He led the way to the sitting room and rather than sitting beside her, he took a seat in a comfortable wing chair in front of the window.

"I'm not sure how to say this," he said. His gray eyes did not meet hers and a silence fell over them.

"What is it?" Penny said. "You're starting to scare me. If something's the matter, please, just tell me."

"I wasn't sure how to tell you this, but I've been playing golf this week with Fiona. Fiona Barton. You remember her. We met her when she came to Llanelen with Alan and Dorothy." When he said her name, Penny's heart sank and she knew what was coming next.

"Yes, I know who she is," she said.

"Look, you've always been honest with me about your feelings, and now, I guess it's my turn to be honest with you about mine. I had hoped that you and I would have something together, something more than what we do have, to be honest. And you've always known that. I think at one time you thought we could, and I think you tried, but whatever 'it' is, it just isn't there. We just don't have 'it.'"

"That's true," said Penny, unsure why her heart was pounding and her mouth was dry. She tried to lick her lips.

"Oh, I know you're fond of me, and we have a wonderful friendship, but that's all we have, and all we're ever going to have," Gareth said. Inwardly, Penny acknowledged the truth of that. "I think you have a deeper wound than you've ever been able to admit, even to yourself, about Tim,"

Gareth said, "and I think it gets in the way of your forming an attachment with another man. Or at least," he said with a tiny shrug, "with me."

His unexpected reference to the death of Tim Crawford felt like an emotional ambush walloping her in the gut. When she was in her thirties, Penny had been engaged to Tim, and watched helplessly one summer afternoon as the River Conwy swept him away after he had gone in to save a drowning child.

"And you want something more," said Penny.

"Yes," said Gareth, "I've realized that I do. This isn't complete."

"But we'll stay friends, I hope," said Penny.

"Always," he said with a simple smile.

"So what are you going to do now?" Penny asked, knowing the answer.

"Well, Fiona invited me to visit her in Edinburgh, so I told her I'd mention it to you, and get back to her."

Penny tilted her head to the side and pursed her lips. "You said you'd talk to me?"

His composure slipped as he let out an embarrassed laugh. "Well, this is all new to me and I wasn't sure how to react or what to do. She knows how close we are and how much I value your friendship."

"And what if I said I wasn't comfortable with your going there?" He did not reply, but he didn't need to. His answer lay silently between them. "Then of course you must go, and I hope everything works out for you."

She smiled warmly at him, the tension melted away, and he breathed a sigh of relief.

"Man, am I glad that's over," he grinned. "I was dreading this conversation. Still, it's early days and who knows what will happen. Now tell me what's been going on around here. You mentioned you've got something to show me connected to the skeleton found in the Gwrych rose garden."

"Yes," said Penny, trying to set aside the emotional impact of what he had just told her. "I've been dying to tell you all about this. I think I know who the victim was, and how she came to be buried there. But I don't know how she died, or the names of who killed her or why. But they might have been gardeners."

She recounted the story of the boy who worked in the Gwrych garden as told to her by Dilys and showed him the letter written by Enid Roberts inquiring after her daughter, Gladwys.

"You can see how worn the creases are," she said. "This meant something to Annie. She must have unfolded it and read it many times. I believe the skeletal remains found in the rose garden are those of Gladwys Roberts."

"After all this time, we may never know who killed her, or why," Gareth said, "and unfortunately it's far too late to bring him or them to justice. They'll be long dead. But it would be a good thing if at least the remains can be positively identified. If this is Gladwys, and it seems likely it is, we even have an old address for her, so it may be possible to find relatives and inform them what happened to her."

"Dilys said that the gardener mentioned that your grandmother tried very hard to find out what happened to her friend," Penny said. "I think you should take this on. You should be the one to find out if there are any relatives and then it would be wonderful if you were the one to inform them."

"You mean I finish what my grandmother started."

"Exactly."

He nodded. "I think you're right."

After a gentle good-bye, he picked up the suitcase containing his grandmother's belongings and drove off. Penny watched his car disappear down the lane and then rang Victoria.

"It's me," she said. "Something's happened. I need to talk to you, but not on the phone. Can you come round?"

"Tea or drink?" Penny asked Victoria half an hour later.

"Which one do I need?"

"Drink." Penny poured them each a glass of white wine and handed one to her friend. Victoria sat on the sofa and curled one leg under her. Penny sat in the chair Gareth had recently occupied.

"What's happened? You look a little shaken."

"I am, a bit. Something's happened and I'm not sure what to make of it."

"Well, tell me and we'll talk it through."

"It's Gareth. Remember I told you about this Fiona Barton who visited with Alan and Dorothy. Well, apparently she and Gareth hit it off and she's the one he was playing golf with. I don't know where they were playing golf, but she's invited him to Edinburgh to visit her and he's going."

"Wow." Victoria took a hefty gulp. "And how do you feel about that? Are you upset?"

"No, I don't think so. Not really. Well, maybe just a little."

226

"Why?"

"I don't know. Because I didn't see this coming? Although, maybe now, come to think of it, I did. That night when we looked through his grandmother's things, he seemed kind of anxious to be away. I thought he was just being emotional, but I wonder now."

"I think this is better for both of you, actually."

"You do?"

"I do. You wanted different things from the relationship. He wanted more than you could give. You were always honest with him and never led him on. I think sometimes you were confused about what you wanted, but he stuck it out. And now he's finally realized that he's never going to get the full relationship with you that he wanted, so when Fiona came along, and the two of them hit it off, apparently, well . . ."

"Yes, you're right, of course. It wasn't fair of me to expect him to stick around for what we had. Still, I thought he was devoted to me, and I didn't really expect this."

"No, of course you didn't. And I think he is still devoted to you and that you two are very close friends, and maybe even always will be, but that's all. And that's okay. That's all you ever wanted, anyway, isn't it?" While Penny mulled that over, Victoria continued, "What do you think of her, by the way? This Fiona."

"I don't know her at all," Penny said. "But I like her well enough, I guess. She seems worthy of him, if you know what I mean. But the funny thing is, as soon as he said her name, I knew he felt something for her. There's just this way people have of saying the name of someone they're interested in."

"In the early stages," agreed Victoria. "The name just drips off the tongue, like honey."

Penny laughed. "I'm not sure it was quite like that, but fair enough. It's almost as if there's a sweet, secret pleasure in just saying the name."

"Still," said Victoria, "you seem to be taking it pretty well."

"That's because I care enough about him to want him to be happy. And by happy, I mean fulfilled. We had, or have, or whatever, a solid, comfortable friendship with deep affection, but it's not romantic, and it looks like he wants a future with someone he can have that with."

"You know," said Victoria, "I'm not sure his involvement with Fiona is really going to change the nature of your relationship with him. Except he might not be around quite as much."

"Time will tell, won't it?"

Penny peered at Victoria's wine glass. "Ready for a top up?"

"No thanks. I'm driving. But you go ahead."

Penny poured a little more wine into her glass. "I do like my own space, and to be honest, when I arrived home today and found him working out back and thought he'd used my key to get into my house, without my permission, I was a bit upset. Felt invaded, but I didn't like the idea of having to talk to him about it."

"So he saved you the bother?"

"No, it wasn't like that. I'd left the back door unlocked—which Gareth wasn't too pleased about—and he was out there planting climbing roses against the back wall. I don't think he'd even been in the house, he just opened the door to let Harrison out. Still, you know what I mean. I never gave him a key, which is an invitation to come and go as he pleased, so thinking he'd used the spare key to let himself in . . . well, that's different."

"It is." Victoria was silent. "By the way, it's just occurred to me that you might want to rethink leaving a spare key under a flower pot or beside a bush or wherever it is. That's just asking for trouble, these days."

"That sounds like something Gareth would have said. Still, it was awfully sweet of him to plant those roses. Especially before he told me he was going to Edinburgh. I mean, what kind of man does that?"

"A lovely man?"

Penny raised her glass slightly. "Here's to Gareth."

Victoria tipped hers. "To Gareth."

Victoria drained the last of her wine and smiled. "What say we go out for dinner? My treat. And you can bring me up to speed on what's been happening at Gwrych Castle. Fancy a curry?"

"No thanks. I'm not British. You know I hate curry."

"Fine. Suit yourself. I know a nice little Italian place."

Twenty-six

"I'd hoped Gareth would have wanted to talk about the John Hardwick mystery," said Penny, "but he probably would have just said we have to wait for the toxicology results to see if my lead poisoning theory holds up. I think he's lost interest in it, to tell you the truth."

"His mind may be on other things," Victoria agreed. "Like Edinburgh."

"Well, my mind's on getting to the bottom of what happened to John Hardwick. So next I need to talk to this Angela Livingstone." Penny dipped a piece of crusty bread into the little saucer of olive oil. "She's the one who signed up to do volunteer work at Gwrych, hung about for a few days, then disappeared. And then, when I spoke to Christina—that's the second Mrs. Hardwick—she told me that Angela used to be a friend of the first Mrs. Hardwick, and they had a particularly nasty falling out. Angela rings Christina every few days asking if there've been any developments in the investigation into the death of John Hardwick and sometimes they meet up. Christina says she's turned into a nuisance and wishes she'd leave her alone."

The waiter appeared with their entrees.

"Oh, it's the fettucine Alfredo for me, thanks," said Victoria.

"And I'm the lasagna."

They picked up their forks and as they started to eat, Victoria said, "Look, I've just had an idea. Why don't we take tomorrow off, or the morning at least, and see if we can find this Angela Livingstone."

"What a great idea. Are you sure you're okay with taking a bit of time off?"

"Why not? They can manage without us at the Spa for a few hours. Maybe even a whole day. We're not that indispensable. Now all we have to do is figure out where to start."

"Well it shouldn't be too hard to find her," said Penny, laying her phone on the table. "I've got a copy of her application form and it gives her phone number and address. Of course, she might have given false details, but it's as good a place to start as any. If it turns out she lied on the form, well, we'll cross that bridge when we come to it."

"Do you think we should ring this Angela or just show up at her house in the morning and hope to find her at home?"

"Let's just show up because I don't want to give her time to think about what she's going to say to us. I want to show her the photo of the people up at Gwrych Castle and ask her if she can identify them. Something connects everyone up there and we have to find out what that is. Or maybe I should say something in their past connects them."

"Sounds good. Now we have to decide what we're going to do about dessert. They do a lovely spumoni ice cream here."

"I really shouldn't."

"Let's share one, then."

"Okay. You talked me into it."

"So where are we off to, then? What's her address?"

"She lives in Llanddulas, which is interesting because that's where the mother of Gladwys Roberts lived."

"Small world."

"It is around here, that's for sure."

The dense Virginia creeper that shrouded the Llanelen teahouse was tinged with the faintest trace of its autumnal red as they drove out of town and along the narrow country roads, flanked by stone walls and green fields, which would bring them to Llanddulas, a village close to Gwrych Castle.

The village is typical of many of its size; a couple of churches, small shops, and a pretty pub. A few streets of identical grey stone houses with charcoal roofs seeming all the greyer on an overcast day, branched off the main street and it was to one of these that the GPS directed them. They pulled up outside the house, and after checking the address against the one on the application form, Victoria switched off the engine.

"What now?" she said.

Penny checked her watch. "It's just past ten. I guess we should see if anybody's home and if we've got the right house."

"Should we go together, or should I wait here?"

"Why don't you wait here until we see how things are?"

Penny walked up to the front door and not seeing a door bell or knocker, lifted the flap on the letter box and banged it a couple of times. Its metallic clanging resounded through what she expected would be a small entry hall. A moment later, at the sound of approaching footsteps, she braced herself for the door to open.

"Yes?" The woman who answered the door appeared to be in her late forties. Her untidy hair, of a washed out, reddish colour, was piled on top of her head and caught up in an inexpensive wide-tooth clip, with a few messy strands hanging down to one side. She wore no makeup and the deep crevices in her face, especially the lines round her mouth, gave her away as a smoker of long standing. She wore a pair of scruffy brown slippers with a large hole in each toe, a pair of grey leggings that looked one size too small, and a long-sleeved cotton top with a V-neck. She had a hard look about her, as if she'd seen a thing or two in her life.

Before Penny could respond, the woman asked, "Are you from the police?"

"No, no," smiled Penny. "Nothing like that. I was doing some paintings up at Gwrych Castle and thought I saw you up there recently. May I come in?"

"What's this about?" The woman kept a firm hand on the door and from her rigid stance Penny expected it to close in her face at any moment.

"It's about John Hardwick. I want to ask you a few questions. You are Angela Livingstone, aren't you?" Penny wondered how many times the woman had heard 'I presume?' after her name, and each time it was spoken the speaker thinking it the most original witticism imaginable.

A cold flash of something indefinable—fear, perhaps?—crossed her face.

"You'd better come in," she said. "But not for long. He'll be back soon."

"Who'll be back soon?"

"My partner."

She led Penny into a cluttered, dusty sitting room filled with overstuffed furniture that had seen better days. She sat down in a saggy chair beside an overflowing ashtray and pointed at the settee. The air was dense with stale cigarette smoke and Penny realized this was going to be a short conversation. Rather than sitting, she remained by the woman's side.

"You are Angela Livingstone, aren't you?" Penny repeated.

"Yes."

"I have a couple of photographs I'd like to show you. They were taken up at Gwrych Castle in the 1990s. I wondered if you could identify some of the people in them." Penny handed her the photos.

"Where on earth did you get these?" Angela asked.

"From a friend," Penny replied.

"Oh, 'from a friend.' I see. Like that, is it? Right well, the big man is Delaney, and that's his dog. And this one," she indicated one of the men, "that's John Hardwick. So now you've got what you came for."

"And who's the other man?" Penny asked. "The one with the cigarette in his hand. Is that Ifor Jones?"

"It is."

"And the woman? Do you know who that is?" Angela did not reply, but gave a slight shake of her head.

"And now I think you'd better leave," she said. "It would be better if you weren't here when he got back."

"When who gets back?"

"Ifor."

"Ifor Jones?"

"He's my partner."

"But if he's your partner, why did you fill out a volunteer form at Gwrych Castle? Surely he'd know who you are."

"Because Mark Baker was on site that day and saw me talking to Ifor. So we pretended I was there to volunteer and I had to fill out a form because Mark insists on everything being done properly."

"But what were you doing up there?" Penny asked. "Why couldn't you just be there as Ifor's partner? Why did you have to pretend to be a volunteer? It doesn't make sense."

"What difference does it make now?" demanded Angela, "and really, what business is it of yours? Although I suppose you made it your business and that's how you found me."

She led the way into the hall, opened the door, and stood to one side. Penny thanked her, brushed past, and walked to Victoria's waiting car.

As Penny sank into the passenger seat, Victoria exhaled heavily and lowered the window.

"You smell like an ashtray," she asked as they drove off. "How'd it go?"

"I got a really bad feeling in there," Penny replied. "Something's not right. She's afraid of something or some-

236

one. I'm certain that the answers to all our questions are to be found at Gwrych Castle. I'm going back to do one more painting."

"Today?"

"No, not today. I need to think how to approach this."

Twenty-seven

One good thing that had thrived from earlier, happier times was the meadow of wildflowers halfway between the block of buildings that comprised Gwrych Castle and a tower that stood about half a mile away down a deeply rutted footpath. Lady Emily's Tower, as it was called, had been constructed as a retreat for the original builder's Georgian bride, and it was here that she reportedly went over the course of her marriage to read and paint. As the years wore on, she was joined by her children, and then her grandchildren, one of whom, Winifred Cochrane, Countess of Dundonald, was the last member of the original family to call the castle home.

Penny gazed upon the field of flowers—white cowslips, yellow meadow buttercups, white ox-eye daisies, red field poppies, and blue forget-me-nots, interspersed among tall wild grasses fanned by a light breeze—and wondered if Lady Emily herself had also painted these same flowers.

She swished her brush in the little jar of clean water and, breathing in the air that had almost a dusty quality from the abundance of late summer plants surrounding her, she began to paint. A gentle buzzing sound reminded her that the field was filled with bees and of course, back in the day when the estate was fully functioning, there would have been bee hives. She pictured the countess in her breakfast room, drizzling honey over her morning toast while she sipped her tea and read the morning newspaper.

Focused on her work, Penny did not hear anyone approaching and was startled when a voice behind her remarked, "Your boyfriend's not with you today, then." It wasn't a question.

She turned to see Ifor Jones, arms folded, in a high-visibility orange-and-red vest. Something in his stance alarmed her. She stood up and looked around but knew there would be no one nearby.

"No, he's not."

"Did anyone give you permission to be here?" Jones demanded.

"I didn't think I needed it. I'm not anywhere near the main buildings."

"You always need it. You're trespassing. So you'd better pack up your things and get out of here."

Penny tipped the water out of the glass jar, screwed on the lid, and placed it in her painting kit. When everything was packed, she folded her easel and tucked it under her arm.

"Right, then. I'll be off. And I'll certainly be having a word with Mark Baker about the manner in which you spoke to me."

"You do that." Jones did not move. Her heart beating savagely, Penny took a step forward and motioned for him to step aside to let her pass. He did and after a moment's hesitation, she began to pick her way along the path that led to the main area.

As a rough hand grabbed her from behind and another covered her mouth, she realized her mistake. She should have listened to her instincts and not left herself vulnerable to him grabbing her from behind.

She kicked backward but missed and he wrestled her to the ground.

She tried to cry out but his hand on her mouth acted like a muzzle.

"Look. Just keep quiet and you won't get hurt," he hissed, releasing his hand from her mouth.

"What do you want?" Penny whimpered. "Let me go. You're hurting me."

"I want you to stop nosing around, asking questions. None of this is any of your business. Don't bring the police in. Now get up. Slowly. Do as I say. Keep your hands where I can see them."

"Just tell me one thing. What happened to the marble staircase? I know you were part of the gang that stole it."

Jones laughed, a harsh, menacing sound that ended in a raspy cough. When the coughing fit had passed, he stood up and looking down at her, said, "It's hidden in plain sight. You may already have seen it, for all I know."

"Okay. I'm just going to get my art supplies. I need them.

If I leave them in this field I'll never find them again." She reached out and grabbed the handle of the canvas bag and pulled it to her. She glanced up at Jones, who was scanning the field, looking back toward the main castle building. Penny reached into the canvas bag and pulled out the small glass jar that had held her brush-cleaning water. She slipped it in the pocket of her jacket and using her hands for balance, got to her knees and then rose slowly to her feet.

"I've hurt my knee," she said. "I can't bend over. Would you get my easel for me?"

As Jones bent over, she smacked the top of the glass jar on a small rock embedded in the rough path and jammed the broken glass into the back of his neck.

"What the . . ." he cried out, as she took off down the path, her canvas bag swinging at her side. If only I can make it to the woods before he recovers, she thought. If I can do that, I can make my way through the woods to the main castle site where there are sure to be people working.

As she began to veer off the path she realized that someone was running toward her, waving. Oh, thank God, she thought. As the figure got closer, she recognized the long hair and realized it was Lane.

"I called him, Penny," he shouted to her. "I saw you up here and saw Mr. Jones throw you to the ground. I figured you needed help so I called him!"

By now Lane had reached her. She threw her arms round him and hugged him.

"Oh, boy, am I glad to see you. Who did you call?"

"I called Mr. Davies. He gave me his card and said I was to call him if I needed help. Well I don't need help, but you do. He said he couldn't come, but he would send someone."

"Oh, that's brilliant!" Penny exclaimed. "You're brilliant. Now we'd better get out of here." Jones lumbered out of the tall grass, holding a bloodied hand to the back of his neck, and lurched off in the opposite direction. Lane stared after him.

"What should we do? Should we try to stop him?"

"No, let him go. He won't get far. He knows it's all over. We'll leave him to the police."

The flashing blue lights of a police vehicle being driven at high speed on the A55 passed far below them and they headed for the main buildings of the castle.

Twenty-eight

Det. Inspector Bethan Morgan was waiting for them when they arrived, and after being assured that Penny and Lane were fine, asked if they felt up to talking about what had happened.

"I don't want to talk here," Lane said. "I don't like it here anymore. And I want to talk to Penny, not you."

"Would you like to go into town and we can all talk there?" Bethan asked. "Penny can be with you, if that's what you want, but I do need to talk to you. I could drive the three of us in the police car. Have you ever been in a police car? Would you like to sit up front with me or in the back?"

"Up front, please," said Lane climbing in.

"I don't know how he'd be at the police station. He might find it too scary," said Penny.

"It really should be the police station," said Bethan, "so we can record it."

"He won't open up there. He likes the café on the square. Could we talk to him there or is that too public?" She answered her own question. "No, that's no good. The place is too cramped and the tables are too close together. Too public. It won't work."

"No, it won't."

"Right, well how about you get him a takeaway coffee from the café, and we meet in the churchyard? We can sit on a bench facing the river, it's peaceful and he'll feel safe there. And it'll be quiet and private."

"Okay. And I'll let his mother know. She may want to be there and if he wants her there, he may be more forthcoming."

Seated on a bench in the churchyard overlooking the peacefully flowing River Conwy, Lane sipped the latte Bethan had bought him. A pair of swans drifted idly under the bridge and tourists eating ice cream sat outside the teahouse opposite. Lane waved to them and they waved back. He grinned at Penny who sat on the low stone wall opposite him, her back to the river.

"I've never been before. Maybe I could come back again. It's nice here."

"It is nice," agreed Penny. "I come here quite a bit, but I work nearby, so it's easy for me. Now Inspector Morgan here has some questions she'd like you to answer. Are you ready?"

"Sure."

"And are you quite certain you don't want your mother with you? It's all right with us if you'd like to have her here."

"No."

"Right, then," said Bethan. "But I still have to call your mother and let her know we're having this conversation. Now, can we start by talking about something that happened just before your dad died? You heard someone arguing with your father and you were scared. Is that correct?"

Lane nodded. "Do we have to talk about this? I don't want to."

"Well, not if you really don't want to, but it would be helpful if you would. Can you just tell me who threatened your father?"

Lane shook his head. "I don't know. It was a woman, though. I know that much. I saw her but I don't know her."

"And can you tell me what they said? Your dad and this woman."

As Lane's hands began to tremble, Bethan reached out and took the coffee from him.

"They were having an argy-bargy my dad and her. Really going at it, they were. And my dad said something like, 'It's not up to me. I'm just getting to know him myself.' And the woman said, 'I should have killed you back then when I had the chance.' And my dad said, 'Well, you won't get the chance now because today's my last day. After today, I won't be back.' And the woman said, 'That's okay. I've already taken my chance.' And then my dad said, 'What are you doing here after all this time? Why can't you just leave the lad alone?' And the woman said 'Because he's my son, that's why.' And that was the last I heard."

Bethan finished writing this down and then exchanged a worried glance with Penny.

"And who do you think they were talking about, Lane?"

His eyes filled with tears. "Me," he said. "They were talking about me."

"And where were they when all this was going on?"

"They were standing just outside the dog kennels."

"And where were you?"

"I was in that little room with the ledge."

"That same room you showed Mr. Davies and me where you spent the nights when you went missing and everyone was so worried about you?" Penny asked.

Lane nodded.

"And when did you hear them arguing?" Bethan asked. "Was it, say, a week before your dad died?"

"No, not that long. Maybe it was the day before," Lane said. "And then after he died, I saw her again in the town and I thought she was looking for me and that's why I didn't want to go home and I got on the bus and went back to the castle. Because she knows where I live and she might have been coming to get me and take me away from Mum and I didn't want that."

"And are you sure you don't know who your dad was talking to?" Bethan asked. Lane shook his head. "Something's puzzling me. If you don't know who the woman is, how could she know where you live?"

Lane looked at her with a confused intensity. "Everybody knows where I live. Even you know where I live. Mum told me that you came to my house and looked in my room."

"Well, that's true. Now let's go back and talk about this

woman. Can you describe her for me? Can you tell me what she looked like?"

"She looked old and wore her hair up on top of her head."

"Angela Livingstone," muttered Penny.

Bethan gave her a quick nod of acknowledgement, then handed Lane's coffee back to him. "I'd like you to tell me about your father's coffee. He liked coffee and brought one with him each morning, is that correct?" Lane nodded and took a sip of his drink. "And what did your father do with this coffee?"

"He had it in his hand like this," Lane held out his coffee, "and he set it down on the little table outside the big green shipping container and then he went in the container and got his tools and high-viz jacket on, then he came out and picked up his coffee and took it with him to work."

"And were other people around at the time?"

"Sometimes."

"But they were busy and took no notice of his coffee, I'm guessing."

"That's right. Why would they?"

"Now Lane, I'm going to ask you a really important question and you can take your time about answering it. Did you ever see anyone put anything in your dad's coffee?"

He dutifully thought for a moment, then shook his head. "No. Why would someone do that? It came just the way he liked it."

"And how did he like it?" Penny asked.

"He liked it sweet. I had a sip once. It was too sweet for me. I like mine with no sugar." His eyes darted toward the teahouse. The people he had waved to a few minutes earlier had left.

"Okay, Lane, that's all for now. You did great. Thank you. You've been very helpful. Would you like me to drive you home?"

"No, it's okay. I want to sit here for a bit and when I'm ready to go home I've got my bus pass." He patted his pocket.

Bethan's phone rang and she stood up and turned her back while she answered it.

"They've picked up Ifor Jones," she said. "I have to go. We've got a lot of questions for him. Thanks for your help today, Penny."

When Bethan was a little way up the the path that led to the gate, Penny turned to Lane. "I'll just sit here for a few minutes with you, Lane, if that's all right. I meant to ask you about the library book. The book on Gwrych Castle that was in your room. The carpet had been coloured in with a red marker. Did you do that?"

"Yeah."

"Well, you do know you're not supposed to write or colour in library books. It's called defacing and the librarians take a dim view of it."

"I don't know what that means."

"It means they don't like when people do that. But the thing is, that book doesn't circulate, which means it can't be checked out and taken home. It's only to be used in the library and yet it was in your room. But I don't think you took it, did you?"

"No, my dad did. I was going to return it for him, but I never did."

"Why do you think he took it?"

"He likes that sort of thing. He reads books about old

buildings and gardens and treasure. He just wanted to know more about the place."

"Well, not to worry. It's been returned." Lane frowned and refused to meet her eyes.

"Is there something you wanted to add?" she asked. "Is there anything else you want to tell me that you didn't feel comfortable telling the police officer?"

"Well, I don't know if it's important or not, but there was a man my dad didn't like."

"And who was that?"

"Mr. Jones, of course. He and my dad used to be friends. Then they had a row about something, and then a falling out and then they weren't friends for a long time and then they met up at the castle again, but they didn't get to be friends again. They weren't nice to each other."

"Well that happens sometimes, doesn't it, Lane?" *Lane.* "Lane. That's an unusual name. Is it short for something?"

"Yeah. My real name's Delaney. It was my mother's what do you call it, something name."

"Maiden name?"

"Yeah, that's right. It was her name before she married my dad."

"Lane, do you remember spending some time up at the castle with your mum and your grandfather? No, you probably don't, because you were only just very small, but by any chance do you remember being there?"

"No, I don't remember being there, but yeah, I know I was. My mum told me. She said it was a happy time in her life. She said she couldn't think of any other place where she'd rather be. Or something like that."

Twenty-nine

"Ifor Jones and John Hardwick were definitely not on friendly terms at Gwrych Castle," Penny concluded at the police station later that day as she recounted the conversation she'd had with Lane after Bethan's departure.

"No, they weren't. Ifor Jones went to prison in the late 1990s for drug possession. A lot of marijuana. He said he was framed. That someone hid it in his car and then tipped off the police. But the police weren't tipped off. He was picked up for drink driving, and the stash was discovered in his car. As for whether someone put the marijuana in his car," she shrugged, "maybe they did. He was convinced that John Hardwick had done it and he waited a long time for his revenge."

"Talk about a dish best served cold."

"The two didn't live close to each other and Hardwick managed to stay out of Jones's way until he started volunteering at the castle to be close to his son. He probably thought that after all this time Jones would leave him alone. I doubt he suspected he was in danger," said Bethan.

"And of course Jones had access to lead. He knew how dangerous lead is. He was a building contractor, so he's worked with it. It's a slow-acting poison, and has to be administered a wee bit at a time so that's what Jones did. He probably used the lead acetate, which has a very sweet taste, and added a tiny amount each morning to Hardwick's coffee. Hardwick liked it really sweet and wouldn't have noticed. Over the course of about six weeks poor John Hardwick got sicker and sicker, until he died. And the doctor couldn't determine what was wrong with him. The symptoms are vague and could be a lot of things. It all makes sense now," said Penny.

"We suspect Jones was with him when he died and stashed the body in the kennel," said Bethan. "Our theory is that he planned to hide it there until dark, and then come back for it and bury it somewhere in the grounds. He thought everybody had gone home for the day but you came along and found the body before he could dispose of it. We'll get to the bottom of it as the interviewing continues."

"If Jones had managed to bury Hardwick's body, who knows? Although the woman's skeleton that was discovered in the garden isn't related to Hardwick's death, maybe there would have been an awful similarity. Maybe Hardwick's body would have lain there for decades and then ninety years or so from now someone would come along and discover it."

Penny opened her handbag and took out the photos that

Jimmy's friend had taken with his new camera at Gwrych Castle in the 1990s.

"Here, you're going to need these. Let me tell you who they are and why they're important. This is the gang that stripped the castle in the 1990s. The fireplaces, all the architectural details, roof slates, paneling . . . everything." Penny pointed out Delaney, the boss of the operation, and then the two younger men.

"I think you'll find if you enlarge this photo that the man here is holding a red packet of Dunhill cigarettes. Gareth found a pack in the fireplace and the company can probably date it for you from the design. And there's a half-smoked one in the packet, which might even have Ifor Jones's DNA on it. And this man," she placed her index finger on the other one, "is John Hardwick. And the woman I thought was his first wife is actually Angela Livingstone and the baby on her hip is Lane. Although John Hardwick is his father, she's actually his mother and sometime during this period she gave him up to Hardwick and his first wife.

"Poor Lane was terribly upset when he overheard Angela say she's his mother and when he saw her in town he thought he was going to be taken away from the woman he knows as his mother. That's why he ran away."

"Well, thank you for helping us wrap everything up, Penny. Appreciate it."

"I wasn't sure you wanted my help. Thought you'd rather do it on your own."

"I did feel that way, at first, and then I thought, well, if all of us working together get the job done, then let's do it. After all it's the result that matters." She closed the file.

"And Gareth. Have you heard from him?" Penny asked.

"No. You?"

Penny shook her head.

The reframed painting of a series of pointed, ivy-covered arches at Gwrych Castle that had been damaged on quiz night, now well wrapped in cushiony protection, leaned against Penny's desk.

"Ready when you are," called Victoria. Penny picked up the painting and the two locked the Spa door behind them, and opened the creaking gate. I must oil those hinges, thought Penny as they walked to Victoria's car.

Penny always enjoyed a drive through the lush Welsh countryside. Fields in contrasting shades of green, neatly bounded by stone walls, sloped away from the road, and gradually blended into the hills. She lowered the window and let the rush of warm air wash over her face. As the car slowed to turn into the lane that led to Heather Hughes's house, a rider on a brown horse trotted toward them. Penny and Victoria waved at Heather's daughter, Jessica, out for her evening ride.

"I don't think I've seen Jessica since we did the preparations the morning of her wedding," Penny remarked. "Eirlys looked after Jessica while I did Heather's nails. Remember our first visit to the house when we did the consultation? We couldn't get over how stunning everything was. So tasteful and modern."

"And functional," said Victoria. "The coffeemaker alone!"

And in the sharpness of the moment, with blinding clarity, recalling how she and Victoria had exclaimed over the beauty of the recently renovated downstairs rooms that had been designed and executed to magazine-perfect quality, Penny understood what Ifor Jones had meant when he'd said, "You may already have seen it for all I know."

Victoria parked the car in front of the stone farmhouse and they crunched their way across the gravel to the front door. They didn't need to ring the bell; Heather opened it immediately and invited them in.

"Here you go," said Penny, handing Heather the painting. "Safely delivered. Finally."

"Wonderful," said Heather. "Thank you. I was waiting until this one arrived to hang the rest. I'm not sure yet where the best place for them would be."

"Maybe I can help with that," said Penny. "Would you mind if I had a look around?"

"No, not at all," said Heather. "Victoria and I'll be in the kitchen having a coffee."

With her heart beginning to beat faster, Penny made her way upstairs to the first floor and finding herself faced with a carpeted hallway that led in two directions and unsure which way to go, she turned to her right. She peeked into a few bedrooms, some with modern but ordinary en suites, until she reached the end of the corridor.

She rested one hand against the door and then pressed the lever. The door opened slowly, and she advanced into the room. The bathroom was spacious and featured a large walk-in shower, and a graceful soaking tub in front of the window, which overlooked a beautifully manicured garden in full bloom.

A chandelier hung from the ceiling. But what stopped her cold was the breathtaking expanse of floor to ceiling marble.

"The steps were of Porto Venere, a type of white Italian marble with purple-and-black striation," Penny whispered, quoting from *The Rise and Fall of Gwrych Castle*.

She'd found it. She was looking at it. The marble staircase from Gwrych Castle, or at least what remained of it. Just as he'd waited years to extract his revenge from John Hardwick, Ifor Jones had waited years for the right project to come along so he could install the stolen marble.

"I didn't want a marble bathroom. It never occurred to me." Penny turned to see Heather in the doorway, with Victoria peering over her shoulder. "And when Ifor Jones first suggested it, I resisted. It seemed too masculine. Too much like something you'd find in an old hotel or maybe even on a ship like the *Queen Mary*. It didn't appeal to me at all. But he was persistent. He could get his hands on some beautiful old marble of exceptional quality and mix it in with new, he said. So finally I gave in. And I must say when I saw it installed, I was stunned. Even the step that leads to the tub is marble."

Penny lowered herself onto the marble step and caressed it as she gazed at the walls.

"It's amazing," said Penny. "I can't believe this is really it."

Heather looked confused. "Really what?"

"This is what remains of the missing marble staircase from Gwrych Castle. I'm sure of it. If you look closely, you can tell the old pieces. They're highly polished, but have a slightly older, yellowish look."

She waved a hand around the bathroom in an airy gesture that took in the scope of the room. "It's not every house that could handle a room like this. Or, to be blunt, everyone who could afford a renovation like this. I'm sorry it was lost, but I'm glad it's been found, here, with you."

She stood up.

"Heather, I have a dear friend, an elderly man, who was up at Gwrych when this marble was stolen. He didn't take part in the theft, but he knows someone who did. My friend feels bad about it. He wishes he'd done something to prevent the theft and desecration that went on up there. I wonder—would you consider allowing me to bring him here one day to see it? He uses a wheelchair, but if he takes his time, I'm sure he could make it upstairs."

"Yes, of course, we can do that."

Penny found herself grinning. "I've just had the most awful thought. When and if word gets out about the history of your marble bathroom, it might become a tourist attraction. People coming from all over to revisit the glory days of Gwrych Castle."

"Oh, God, I hope not." Heather laughed lightly and then became serious. "You don't think I'll have to give it back, do you?"

"With the new marble mixed in with the old, who's to say for sure what's really yours and what isn't? And even if you could somehow separate the new from the old, who would you give it back to? And if several people or groups came forward to claim it, then what? An expensive court case that nobody can afford and then the marble sits for another fifty years in a warehouse until it's lost and forgotten? What would be the point of that?"

She ran her hand over the marble wall, appreciating its smooth, cool beauty, its history, and imagining it, dressed in its red carpet, in its rightful place as the stunning centrepiece of a magnificent castellated mansion.

"No, Heather, your marble is for keeps."